Contents

REUBEN'S PORTION

By
Josephine Cunnington Edwards

ILLUSTRATED BY JOSEPH W. MALMEDE

TEACH Services, Inc.
PUBLISHING
www.TEACHServices.com ▪ (800) 367-1844

Copyright 1957 © Josephine Cunnington Edwards
Copyright 2018 © TEACH Services, Inc.

ISBN-13: 978-1-4796-0631-3 (Paperback)
Library of Congress Control Number: 2018940359

TEACH Services, Inc.
P U B L I S H I N G
www.TEACHServices.com • (800) 367-1844

Reuben Begins
to Rebuild

REUBEN[1] stood looking up at the gigantic, crumbling shell that had once been his home. Yes, the spirit of the South had been broken by Sherman's terrible march to the sea—that mowing of a swath many miles wide, leaving nothing for the old, the very young, and the helpless. Reuben felt broken, too, as he stood there and looked and wondered what he could do next, where he could turn.

So this was his portion, was it? Was this desolation, this ruin, to be "Reuben's portion"? He remembered his old grandfather explaining to him long ago that *Reuben* meant "unstable as water." Troubled

---

[1]For obvious reasons the names of people, towns, and communities have been changed.

7

at the old man's ominous looks, he asked what *unstable* meant. "Weak—weak as water," he was told. Reuben remembered that when he showed any weakness or indecision in the old man's presence, grandfather would look at him speculatively and muse aloud, "Unstable as water, thou shalt not excel."

Reuben took everything for granted in the old days before the war—horses, leisure, parties, hospitality, fine clothes, plenty of food. The Negroes picked the cotton, and the thousands of bales which the rich soil of "Live Oaks" produced afforded the Pelman family a high standard of living.

Money had also been taken for granted; he thought that there would be enough to pad his future. He had aimed to study law, but the guns at Fort Sumter spoke the very year he was to go. He was one of the first in the county to go to war.

Now it was too late, for there was nothing left —not a thing. His mother died of typhoid fever the first year of the war, and his father died shortly after "Live Oaks" was burned by soldiers going through. Old Cuff, his father's faithful personal servant, had told him briefly of that mournful event. "Yo pa, he jes tuck on lak a chile, seein' de ole place burn up. Sich useless waste of all de yeahs yo pa wuked, and wuked. Marse Reuben, he jes wa'nt de same atter dat—jes pined and mou'ned ontell de win' nigh blowed him away."

With Abe Lincoln dead of an assassin's bullet, the harsh reconstructionists had laid on taxes that he could never hope to pay. He would have to leave old "Live Oaks," where five generations of Pelmans had lived, married, worked, wrought, and died. The little burial acre with its tall gravestones spoke grimly in marble of a proud, honorable, and aristocratic ancestry. But what good did that do him now? He must carve out his own niche; he must found his own dynasty. He must earn and dig out the right to a portion somewhere else.

Standing there, Reuben seemed to see it all as it had been before he had marched away to the war—the miles of cotton, the hum of activity around the slave quarters, the baying of the hunting hounds down at the river bottom.

In the big outside kitchen Aunt Car'line had ruled supreme. She was so fat that she caused a minor earthquake whenever she moved about, but such foods as she concocted there at that gigantic fireplace! Reuben recalled the beaten biscuits—yellow as gold and puffy as the cotton that blew in yonder field. Hominy was often sputtering in its savory juices in the long-legged skillet that squatted over hot coals.

Hungrily, Reuben stood there and tormented himself still further. Even thinking of Aunt Car'line's humble old grits and gravy started the juices flowing in Reuben's mouth. Then there were corn pone; stewed chicken, fixed with rice and gumbo; home-churned butter—crocks and crocks of it, churned sweet in the cool of the spring house, where the cold water flowed around the jugs and crocks, keeping butter solid and milk cool even on the hottest days.

His mother was there too—so dainty, so fragile, and so lovely. Amazingly capable, too, for she kept the vast machinery of a big planter's household running smoothly. Candlelit banquets in the vast dining room were a poignantly sweet memory. Then there were the hoop-skirted belles who used to do the minuet in the lovely ballroom.

10

Reuben looked long at the little implement that had meant so much to his mother.

Standing there in the fading light of the western sun, Reuben thought of his own life and how he must build anew on the ashes of the past. As he turned at last to go, Reuben noticed something in the soil at his feet. He bent over and dug it out of the ground with his forefinger.

It was his mother's tiny gold thimble. He looked at it for a long time. He had seen her wear it scores of times, her quick hands like little white birds flying over fine linen or doing endless dainty stitches on embroidery or intricate quilting patterns. Now the coverlets, the quilts, the stiff-bosomed ruffled shirts, were all as far gone as if they had never been a tangible part of his life.

Rising up quickly, he looked long at the little implement that had meant so much to his mother, so girt about as she was by the many trivialities that compose life. Then, almost grimly, he put the thimble in his pocket. It would be his talisman—the only link tying the old life to the new. On this small beginning he would build again. Reuben would build more solidly than the Cavalier ancestors who thought they had built for the ages. Setting his jaw firmly,

12

Reuben vowed then and there that he would build a life that war, famine, or loss could never sweep away. How he proposed to do this, he did not know.

Reuben had two things that were priceless—his youth and his health. The only thing wrong with him was the chilblains on his feet, from which he suffered every winter. His feet were badly frozen during the third winter of the war while he was in Pennsylvania. He had not realized that cold weather could be so cruel.

Turning on his heel, he went down the long lane of locust trees, which held many memories for him. When he got to the road, he turned north and walked until the moon rode high.

As weariness bore in upon his consciousness until he was forced to heed it, he saw an old barn near the ruins of another big house. He could see hay still bulging out of the windows of the ancient haymow. Almost in a dream, Reuben climbed up the dusty ladder and smoothed the ragged blanket out upon a heap of hay. He had hardly lain down until he sank into a sleep of deep exhaustion—for this was a princely bed compared with some he had slept

13

in since he last slept in the fine old four-poster in his room at Live Oaks, between sheets smelling of rose petals and heliotrope. After mud, rain, snow, and yes, even a blinding blizzard he had fallen asleep in sheer weariness. The matter of waking again was of small moment to him. He awoke, however, breakfastless, with a gnawing akin to pain in his very vitals. Almost like a sleepwalker, he arose, washed in a nearby stream, and started on—where, he did not know.

All that day he walked on, and on, and on. He was not aware of the beauty of the bright and beautiful day, or of the silence and inactivity of the farms and villages he passed. He felt a passing relief that no cannon boomed in the distance and the flames of no battle destruction leaped into the sky.

Once, passing a home where some poor white folks lived, he paid a shinplaster (25¢) for a plate of boiled salt pork cooked with dried peas and goobers (peanuts). They gave him a chunk of corn pone to eat with it, and a whole string of incredibly dirty children stood openmouthed and watched him while he ate.

Because of his great hunger, he could hardly keep from wolfing the food. Even so, the meat must have been spoiled, for he was ill for a good share of the afternoon. With sheer dogged determination, he walked it off. He had lived with pain, hunger, and great discomfort for such a long, long time, that he was almost impervious to an existence where they were not his constant companions. He could always endure; he always had.

Along toward the evening of the fourth day of walking, he spied a building or two of a ruined village, nestled at the base of a lovely green hill. Unaccountably his interest awakened slightly. Nothing he had passed so far had touched him in the least. Toward this he shuffled, suddenly conscious of his horrible shoes with holes in the soles so huge that dirt, gravel, and filth were ground into the soles of his feet. He had worn no socks for a long time. He was conscious of his ragged gray uniform, now polychromatic from battle, blood, sun, rain, mud, and snow.

As he drew near, he perceived that the building he had seen in the distance was a store, or rather had been one, before the devastation of the war had taken its terrible toll. What there was left was patched most inexpertly.

He could not understand why he was attracted to the old place, but he eyed it attentively as he passed wearily along the road. Just as he was almost even with the front porch, an old man came out and proceeded to drag in a few things. Reuben noted with astonishment that it was indeed a store, though he could see very little for sale. In those days stores did not close as early as they do now; they were kept open late. Around the stove many an old fiery social and political problem was roundly discussed and settled as far as that particular community was concerned.

But now bushwhackers—wild, lawless men, like beasts of prey—fed like buzzards on the leanness of the country. No one was safe; everyone was wary and fearful. Acting on impulse, Reuben approached the old man, who was trying with puny strength to edge a barrel of sweet potatoes into the store door. His movements were weak, almost feeble. The young man sprang to help him.

2   "Let me lend you a hand, Sir," he cried, seizing the
barrel and rolling it easily.

"Let me lend you a hand, Sir," he cried, seizing the barrel and rolling it in easily. Five minutes before he had thought he was too tired to lift his feet another step. The old man looked up piteously, his red-rimmed eyes clouded with fear and suspicion for a minute. Then as he looked searchingly into Reuben's eyes, his face cleared.

"Thank ye kindly, Son; thank ye. I ain't as strong as I was once."

Determined to finish what he had started, and still puzzled by his unaccountable interest in the tumble-down old place. Reuben helped the old man close up shop. Indeed a poor excuse for a shop it was. The shelves were practically empty, and what was laid out to sell was so shopworn and so poor that Reuben doubted that it would ever be sold. Then the old man picked up a jug of sorghum molasses and started out the back way toward rooms built onto the back of the store.

Reuben turned toward the road again, but the old man called him back. He spoke hesitantly, again reminding Reuben of a little child—a weary, hurt, and bewildered child.

"I'd take it kindly, Suh, if you'd come and break bread with mother and me. We don't live very good, and we ain't got much to offer to a soldier who fit fer us. Times is hard, Son, and we're lucky to have pone and molasses for supper. There's a lot of folks that ain't got as much."

So Reuben sat between the old people and heard of their two sons who died in the terrible war; of the big store, looted again and again by both armies; of the burning of the store and of the home until the hard work of a busy and useful life lay in ashes at their feet. Their sons—the pride and joy of their lives—lay in unmarked graves on a distant battlefield. Now, feeble and prematurely aged, they were reduced to this ramshackle old building, all that was left of their comfortable holdings.

The old woman had brewed a kind of coffee from something, but Reuben drank it gratefully. The meal for the pone was poorly ground, but even that, eaten at a table and with undeniably strong molasses, was the best meal Reuben had eaten for a long, long time. They all ate without complaint, for they all had known hunger and privation.

19

Even though both of the old people had constant fear in their hearts of all strangers, they both were reluctantly drawn to the young man—as was he, unaccountably, to them. In spite of their fears they urged him to spend the night. Old Mrs. Conners, as Reuben learned her name to be, fixed him a bed on an old decrepit sofa, with patched, clean sheets. The sofa had once been beautiful, stuffed and tufted; but it had been hacked by the swords of the raiders in search for hidden valuables. Once the Connerses had offered their hospitality, they were filled with fear at what they had done, and both of them stayed awake for a long time.

"Myry," the old man whispered in the darkness.

"Yes, Silas," his wife replied.

"I'm a mind to ask him to stay on with us and help us."

"You ain't got nothing to offer him, Pa."

"No, I know I haint, Myry, but just the same he is worse off than we are, exceptin' he's got youth and stren'th. Unless something breaks for us, I don't know what we'll do, and he needs a place to 'light and needs it bad."

"He kind of reminds me of Charlie," the old woman said after a while.

"I thought so, too, Ma. Especially the way he kind of throws back his head when he laughs, quiet-like. You know, Charlie wa'nt never boisterous-like, and noisy, like other fellers around here."

"His teeth are real white and straight, and he's got yeller hair like Charlie, too," the old woman added wistfully, remembering a bonny son who marched away to war gaily and perished at Petersburg.

So it was that two old people, tired of war, tired of trouble and worry, anchored their hopes of a better tomorrow on a soldier boy, who at that moment was sleeping soundly on the first soft spot he had lain down on since he had marched away to war, under the stars and bars, four years before.

Over a meager breakfast the next morning, old man Conners put his strange proposition up to the young soldier. Reuben was amazed at the trust the two put in him. "Why, how do you know that I am honest?" he asked. "How do you know that I am not a renegade, a bushwhacker? I beg of you, do not

21

put your trust in just anyone. Your very lives are in danger!" Reuben looked at the old couple with real concern in his eyes over his breakfast of pone, hominy grits, and sorghum. Old Mr. Conners hesitated a moment before he answered Reuben. Then he raised his childlike blue eyes and looked Reuben full in the face.

"I pride myself, Son, on my ability to read people's characters," he answered simply, his old hand shaking a little as he set down his coffee cup. "Dozens of soldiers have gone this way. Many have broken bread with ma and me. But you are the first one we have seen to make us think of our boys, Charlie and William. I guess, even though we know they are dead, we can't help but watch the road, ma and me. Charlie was light, frangy [fragile], and earnest like you. . . . William, he, well, he had black hair like ma's used to be when she was a girl, and blue eyes. Ma and I could hardly sleep last night, thinking of how you look so much like Charlie used to look."

"But just the same, it is dangerous," Reuben repeated. But the old man interrupted him.

"You just look honest out of your eyes, Son, like our Charlie used to look. Charlie would never have harmed the old and poor."

The upshot of it all was that Reuben stayed on with the old people and was their pride and joy. In his spare time he fixed up one of the other rooms of the ruined building for a bedroom for himself. By repairing—nailing up something here and there and whitewashing—in a short time the store and house combination began to look like a different place.

Then one day Reuben decided to go to a center some forty-odd miles away to get more stock for the store. As he explained to the fearful and timorous old man, they could never expand or grow unless they had some things to sell in the store.

Almost reverently he took the pitiful little savings pa got from under the loose board in their bedroom, overwhelmed by the trust they put in him, a comparative stranger.

Because of the danger and the uncertainty of the times, Reuben took an old road, almost obliterated by weeds and grown over by creeping sod, which pa had told him about. He drove entirely at night, arriving at the little railroad town at dawn on the third day.

Carefully and economically he bought only essentials—the bare necessities for a little struggling populace that, because of terrible hardships, bought only what they could not raise: tea; a little precious dark-brown sugar; coarse salt; several bolts of calico; factory cloth, unbleached and coarse. He got a little saleratus, a few iron cook pots, some long-legged skillets (favored for baking pone), and some iron spoons.

Cautiously he loaded up, knowing full well he could easily be robbed before he was a mile out of town. Then he started out briskly in the direction opposite to the road he actually aimed to take. Out of town, he drove off the road, then got out and led his mule across a wide field and forded a small stream. After a while he found a small woods road, choked with grass, leading in the direction he wanted to go. Then he hobbled the mule, got his blanket out from under the seat, and slept all the rest of the day.

It was getting dusk when he awoke. He carefully kindled a small fire and fixed himself a little food

Men, women, boys, and girls came to see the new merchandise.

before he started out. Two days later, at daybreak, he pulled up in front of Conners's store. Ma and pa both were beside themselves with joy at his return and at the cleverness of his selections and purchases. Highwaymen and ruffians were plentiful in those hard days following the war.

It took the greater part of the day to put up the stock and take care of the things he had brought in —not because there was so much, but because they made an occasion of it. All day men, women, boys, and girls came in to see the new merchandise. Not all came to buy, for the war had taken so much from the people that few had any ready money. But they came just the same. A few brought rugs, wool, dried apples, and chickens to trade for new things. Reuben saw with glistening eyes that he could be loaded both ways the next time he went after stock. Ma and pa were nonplused at the change that had come over their lives.

In two days the shelves were almost empty again, and trade stuff was everywhere. A couple of sheep, some pigs, and a bull calf were in a hastily constructed pen outside; bags of wool were piled up in every corner. A couple of baskets of eggs, some bags of dried and parched corn, and a few dried apples were taken into ma's sitting room because the store-room was so full.

"I'll have to load up and go again," Reuben told pa. "This time I think I'll go about twenty miles farther to Minersboro. It is a bigger place, and there will be more things to choose from and a better market for the things I take to trade."

Ma and pa were afraid again for his safety, but he assured them that not for nothing had he carried dispatches right through the enemy's lines all through the war without ever a scratch. He knew all the tricks. And he had gotten so he could see like a cat— as well in the dark as in the daylight. So off he went again in another direction, again going by unused roads and always at night. Some people said that Reuben knew more of the old unused roads of that part of the state than anyone else.

In the course of six months Conners's store was the best one in that part of the county. People began to move around close and a little village began to take shape. Then one day a doctor came and set up his office and an apothecary shop in a big empty house. Soon a lawyer put out his shingle. It was not long until a returned soldier moved in and set up a blacksmith shop at the end of the village street. Another clerk was hired to help pa, for Reuben had to be on the road more than half the time. Pretty soon a post office grill was set up at one side of the store, and the town of Conners was started.

An Interesting Customer

ONE DAY while Reuben was putting up a newly acquired stock of boots and shoes, the door opened and a strange girl walked into the store. Reuben gawked at her like a yokel. In contrast to the girls round about, she looked like a queen. Her dress looked new and of fine quality bombazine. Great hoops made her look like a gigantic green mushroom. Her black hair was parted in the middle, with tiny bobbing curls at the side of her face. Reuben almost fell off the ladder upon seeing such beauty.

Hastily scrambling down, he went over behind the big cheese he had brought in a couple of days before, and which was covered grandly with mosquito bar, and managed to ask her what she wanted.

29

"Have you silk thread," she asked in a soft, husky, well-bred voice, "I mean a color to match this?" She produced a small piece of bright blue silk. Reuben went and got the box which held the thread. He was overjoyed to find he had a spool that matched the scrap of blue silk cloth exactly.

Before she went out of the store, Reuben managed to find out a great deal about her. She was the daughter of a well-to-do planter whose family had lived a few miles north of Conners, and like many others, had lost nearly all they had. Only that week they had moved what household effects they had saved to a house west of the village, hoping there to retrieve, in some way, the fortune they lost during the war.

The mother, the more ambitious of the couple, had heard of Conners and determined to start a school. The girl's father had investigated the stream flowing through the property they had acquired and declared that he could have a gristmill running there in no time at all. Their name was Seymour; they were of fine old English stock and were fond of boasting about it.

"My aunt, who lives in Ohio, sent me this cloth and some other things," Sabina Seymour had explained to Reuben shyly. "She married a Yankee schoolmaster. My, but I was glad to get some things. I really needed clothes."

"Sabina, Sabina," Reuben whispered to himself after she had gone out. Why, that was the prettiest name he had ever heard of, and she was the prettiest girl he had ever seen. For the first time since he had come home from the war his thoughts began to turn into channels other than the worn grooves of necessity. As in a dream, he methodically and neatly put the stiff, ungainly boots and shoes up into the shelves, to sell to the people who had never seen better.

After a while he brought his thoughts sternly into subjection. Had he not pledged himself by the tiny gold thimble that had once graced his mother's dainty finger that he would build once more? He would build up the old family fortune again. But now, out of the failures, the mistakes of the past, he would build a more enduring structure, one that could not be torn down so easily, as had the one his father and grandfathers built.

31

He would buy back the old acres, now lying fallow, and build another lovely home on the crumbling foundations of the old one. In his dreams the fields bloomed again, green and white, with the miles of growing cotton. In his dreams mules, strong and of fine strain, with rippling muscles, drew wagons loaded with bales and bales of cotton—his cotton— to the barges drawn up to the docks in the stream.

But here Reuben always had to stop and face reality. Who would sow? Who would hoe? Who would pick? Who would run the gin and bale the cotton? The old order had tumbled down and was gone forever, and he did not know the new. With a sigh he climbed down the ladder and began to lift bolts of bright calico, fresh from the mills of New England, and to arrange them on his clean white-washed shelves. Again he felt the sting of despair. How could he order his life? How could he? How could he?

Then, slowly, a plan evolved in his eager brain. The bright dream of rebuying and rebuilding the old plantation must go, dear as it had grown to be. Then with a clarity that amazed him he began to see that he had been wasting his substance on the dreams of a fool. The new life that he desired to build must not be built after the fashion of the old. If it were, it too would fall. Standing there, he looked at the shelves in a new light. A dream almost as tangible as reality came into his heart. He seemed to envision what he would have to do. He must do without everything unnecessary. He must hoard and save all that pa gave him as wages. Save and save and save his precious portion that he was willing to sweat, labor, and work so hard to obtain. Save until the glad hour when he could strike out for himself— with his own store. He would not be unstable as water. This Reuben would excel!

He threw himself into his work with feverish energy and worked from dawn until the moon rose high many a night. He went far afield, for miles and miles around, buying up wool, eggs, chickens, pot cheese, beans, peas, and peanuts. His wagon was on the go continually now, taking in Millerburg, Eckerle, and Gambelia Center.

More people moved into Conners, and more people meant more customers for Conners's store.

The past year had brought an abundant harvest for those who had been able to plant. Things were looking up. There had been plenty of rain, and the whole neighborhood seemed filled to the brim with cheer and hope. More and more money went into the tin box under the loose board in the floor of Reuben's bedroom. Pa could afford to be lavishly generous with him. He realized that all that he had he owed to the industry of the returned soldier boy.

About this time Alger Collinsmith, a nephew of Ma Conners, whose whereabouts had been unknown by his relatives for years, suddenly showed up. He asked for a job as a clerk in the store, which was immediately given him. From the moment of his arrival, Reuben distrusted Alger. He had a sneaky, furtive look and was downright lazy at times. Even pa was distressed, but ma was pleased to have someone of her own kin about, so he was allowed to remain. But things were not quite the same again; both pa and Reuben sensed it. Reuben realized that Alger was almost insanely jealous of his hold on the business, but there was nothing he could do about it. The two were wary of each other and stayed out of each oth-

Ten minutes more and he would have gotten away with it.

er's way. One day Reuben came home from one of his trips a day sooner than was expected. Going quickly up to his room, he came upon Alger kneeling over the loose board and lifting out the tin box with his savings. Ten minutes more and he would have gotten away with it. Outraged, Reuben literally threw the thief out of his room and stormed down to pa with the box in one hand and the accusations on his lips. Pa discharged Alger immediately, for he well knew who had been his friend.

Even ma was fed up with the laziness and the general good-for-nothingness of her sister's son. He spent more time at the taproom in the nearby tavern than he did behind the counter. He let the store get so dirty that it took Reuben a day or two to clean it up between trips. Anyone could see that it was not fair.

When fall came, the Seymours' dream of a school at last materialized. When Pa Seymour had his mill finished, there was enough grist to give him dreams of a lumber mill farther up the river. However, Ma Seymour let him know that the lumber mill would have to wait till her house was put into readiness for the subscription school she was determined to start. So Pa Seymour got busy, and after much activity and commotion in the long drawing room of the house they had bought, arrangements for classes were finished and the date for school was announced. The attendance exceeded her wildest dreams. More children and youth crowded into the big room than could possibly be accommodated.

"Why, I didn't know there were so many children and young folks around here," she told her husband. When he suggested that they cull out a few and send the rest home, she rose mightily to the occasion.

"Not a one of these seekers after knowledge shall be turned away," she declared expansively. So Sabina was pulled into the teaching profession almost against her will. All the smaller children were relegated to the upstairs drawing room, with Sabina installed as the teacher. Pa Seymour was dispatched to the carpenter shed to begin more benches and forms and a new blackboard for Sabina. Sabina had intended to take over the running of the house while her mother taught. Now Aunt Sukey Hipscor, who

lived in the next county, a strong woman—a widow—
was sent for. Ma Seymour was equal to any and
every emergency. So school started auspiciously and
grandly, for she never did anything halfway.

The Seymours had to take foods and farm prod-
ucts as pay for the schooling of the children. They
used as much of the produce as they could, but Conners helped them to sell much of it on consignment.
They took in so many sheep and calves that Pa Seymour fixed up the fences and used livestock as a
side line to his many lucrative ventures. He whistled
while he went about his work. A school, a mill, a
farm, with plenty of livestock. He was living again
after the horrors of the war years.

A fine thing happened that winter. A soldier
named Corbin Croftin came to town and set up his
own carpenter shop; he was something of an artisan,
for the chairs and the tables that came from his shop
were things of real beauty. They are cherished to
this day in the homes of some of the people who
live near Conners. But he was more than a fine
craftsman in furniture, bedsteads, tables, and high-
boys. He was a singer and could also play the violin.

The school had grown so large that it almost was forcing the Seymours out of house and home, so Corbin helped to get behind a drive for a proper schoolhouse. He organized the men and boys, and with the wood from Pa Seymour's sawmill, which he had put in operation, the schoolhouse was up in the matter of a few days. Corbin laid aside his own orders and helped to make more desks and forms that were sorely needed.

One of the first things Corbin did that year was to start a singing school. "I aim to teach singing, fiddle playing, and if anyone's got a melodeon or a harpsichord, I can play on that. My price won't be high." The village got into a fever of excitement. Even in faraway New York, or Boston, could there be more culture than there was right here in Conners?

The singing school proved to be the most popular innovation in the whole countryside. Corbin managed to buy a melodeon and a harpsichord and had them installed in the front of the school. People came from miles around in rigs, and sleds, and lumber wagons, and mudboats, depending on the state of the weather.

It was at this school that Reuben discovered he was the possessor of a fine tenor voice. He and Sabina went to every meeting of the singing school. Sabina helped Corbin by playing the melodeon while he directed the music. Reuben was proud of her and was sure no girl in all the county was as smart as she.

Even Pa and Ma Conners went to the schoolhouse to see and be seen, for it was the social center of the whole county. One night, when Corbin played a particularly lovely piece on the violin, ma cried a little in her handkerchief. After Reuben got in that night, pa stopped him on the way to the stairway and laid a fine old violin in his hands.

"Ma and I would take it kindly, Son, if ye would take Charlie's fiddle and learn to play on it. I drove clear to State City to get it for him the day he was fifteen. I don't think it was ever out of his sight till he marched off to war. Me and ma would like to hear you play it. It ain't new—wasn't new when I bought it. Charlie said the older the fiddle, the better it is. It's yours, Son."

There was a mist in Reuben's eyes when he took the old treasure with reverent hands. His heart was so full he could find no voice to thank pa. One glance into Reuben's face satisfied the old man, and he went his way content.

It was not a year before Reuben was playing the violin remarkably well. Even his teacher was astonished. "Are you sure you never played a violin before?" Corbin asked suspiciously, his eyes on the young man's face.

"Never had one in my hands. But I will say this: I have always loved the violin better than any other musical instrument in the world."

"Well, that could account for it, but I'd swear you'd had lessons before."

"Nope."

"Well, I will say this: It won't be long till you learn all I know, and then some. Going ahead is a matter of application and practice. You're good."

"You are joking with me," Reuben said, his hands caressing the satiny patina of the old instrument.

"No, I'm not," Corbin answered. "I ain't much of a joker. I just don't understand how you can play the fiddle so good, never having had hold of one

41

before. But I reckon it's like makin' fine furniture. You can do a lot better if you throw your heart in it."

"I suppose that is the reason why," Reuben mused. "It must be because I like it so well. When I pick up that fiddle, it just seems like I am in another world. I see things and hear things I never saw or heard before."

Two more years went by on wings. You'd never have known the place now as the ramshackle community Reuben stopped at four years before. The school and a new church building attracted more people. The people had musical instruments of all kinds from zithers to squeeze boxes. Even the school children brought jew's harps to school, and the recess time resounded with their efforts to learn a few tunes on them. A large pianoforte sat in grandeur in the Seymour home. Sabina played it better than anyone else in the neighborhood, even Corbin. Reuben was now twenty-eight years old, the pride and joy of Pa and Ma Conners's hearts.

After his experience with Alger, Reuben had to find another place to hide his savings, for banks were neither safe nor dependable in those days. He never hid it again in the spot that Alger had discovered, for fear he would break in some night while he was on a trip and take all that he had saved up for years. So Pa Conners helped him to find a new place. Behind the store was a room where coal oil was stored, those being the beginning days of the kerosene lamp. In the wall was an old cupboard, but it had a secret panel in it. Pa and he both kept their savings there. And well they did, for several times the place was searched, but never a farthing was found. Reuben and pa both were sure that Alger was at the bottom of it, but they could prove nothing.

Some Serious Discussions

*J*INALLY the day came when pa and Reuben decided that a trip to New York was necessary. Better and also cheaper goods could be had; of that Reuben was convinced. Conners's store was the best mercantile establishment in that part of the state. Partly because of the thriving condition of the village, the railroad was rebuilt and the train came through the town again. The goods he bought in New York could be shipped back cheaper than he could bring them from a much nearer market. The day he left, the small depot was full of friends and well-wishers seeing him off.

"Don't fall afoul any Yankee sharpers, Reub!"

"Watch yer pockets, Reub!"

"See Castle Gardens! See Barnum's Museum! See Sandy Hook and Brooklyn!" With so many interested friends wishing him well, how could he fail?

When Reuben got back some time later, the town had never seen such fine things as graced the shelves of the Conners's store. There were dishes and crockery such as the folk in the war-torn South had not seen in years. He brought one oddity that few had seen. It was a stove called the "Farmer's Favorite." It was fired by wood at one end. It also had a high oven on one side, which (they told him in New York) baked ever so much better and easier than a fireplace could. Most people eyed it dubiously, and many of the women openly scoffed. "As if anything could be better than a good Dutch oven for hoecake!" Or, "It looks dangerous to me. Are you sure it won't explode?"

Then, exasperated, Reuben would explain again the marvelous principles behind what he believed was a truly wonderful innovation. Mrs. Seymour finally bought it and set it up in her big kitchen. Her husband filled the woodbox behind it with scraps from the sawmill. She got so enthusiastic about it (it did

45

not "hot" up the house in the summer, and it would boil up a dinner in a short time with much less effort) that a fever soon developed on the part of everyone in the village to have a Farmer's Favorite.

After Reuben's trip to New York, he had wonderful tales to tell. He had changed trains in Washington and spent the night there. He had walked out to the White House, gotten swept in on a reception of some kind there, and shaken hands with General Grant, who was then president of the United States. Someone had pointed out Ford Theatre, where John Wilkes Booth had shot President Lincoln seven years before.

"One wonderful thing," Reuben told Sabina that day, "was that I got a glimpse of the Grand Duke Alexis."

"Who is he?" asked Sabina curiously. She was far more interested in the poplins, the bombazines, the muslins, and the silks he had brought back than all the celebrities he had seen.

Reuben laughed and put down the two shoe boxes he was holding for Sabina to look at. She seized them eagerly.

"The Grand Duke Alexis," Reuben told her impressively, "is the third son of Czar Alexander of Russia."

Sabina stopped and looked up at Reuben quickly, her eyes big with wonder. "And you saw a real prince, the son of a real king?" she breathed in wonder.

Reuben laughed at her. "Yes, Sabina, a real prince," he answered soberly. "But they tell me there are people there far poorer than we, so his grandeur did not impress me so much. I was more interested in seeing the graves of Robert Fulton, who invented the steamboat, and Alexander Hamilton, who established our money system, than all the grand dukes they could produce."

"Oh, Reuben, is New York interesting?"

"I should say so, Sabina. I wish you could see the ports—big sailing vessels from many nations all along the waterfront. I saw the place where Washington was inaugurated president and where he lived till they changed the capital to Philadelphia."

"I didn't know the national capital was ever in Philadelphia."

"Yes, it was for a time. You know, when I stood there in Trinity churchyard, I thought of how it must have been when the fine procession swept past there and made Washington the president. All of a sudden I realized that in spite of war this is my country, and I love it."

Sabina had taken the lovely brown shoes made of velvet that Reuben had brought, and was rubbing her soft hands over their lustrous surface. "I am glad," she said youthfully, "that we can get things for our houses and ourselves again." Then, as if she realized that the thing she had said was both shallow and selfish, she added quickly, "But I am gladdest about peace and the chance to build a good life on the ashes of the old."

It was then that Reuben climbed down the ladder and went to the counter where Sabina was standing.

"Sabina," he said quietly, his voice vibrant with emotion, "Sabina, that is exactly what I want to do —to build again—to make a life that cannot be broken or ruined like the old way we had before the war."

48

The two of them were alone in the store. It was midafternoon. Pa Conners was resting, and the other clerk was on one of the shorter trips. Trade was always at a standstill during the heat of the early afternoon, so Reuben spent his time in opening his heart to her as he had to no one else. He told her of the ambitions which had consumed him ever since he stood by the stark and ruined walls of his old home several years before.

The girl listened gravely, his own enthusiasm reflected in the glow of her brown eyes. Impulsively excusing himself, Reuben went upstairs to his bedroom and got the tiny gold thimble that he held as a talisman to spur him on to achieve his ambition, or die trying.

Sabina took the little treasure and looked at it curiously. Then she looked up at Reuben. "Then, this is the reason you are so different from most of the other men and boys around here; most of them are either married or promised; but you, Reuben, you are wedded to this little thimble."

Reuben, watching her, realized that it was partly true. She put it on her small shapely finger, held it

4

up, looked at it, then took it off and laid it on the counter before Reuben.

"You will make it if anyone can," she added simply. "Everybody says you have made this town of Conners. People say it ought to have been called Pelman, after you."

Reuben laughed at that. "Oh, no, Sabina, don't think that. All that I am I owe to Pa Conners. He gave me the chance I needed when I needed it. I was hungry, broken in spirit, and in rags. They did not have much, but they did have more than I had, and they divided all they had with me. A person can't ever forget that."

But Sabina would not agree. "All that may be true, Reuben, and we all know that it is. But you have helped pa more than he has been able to help you. Even he says that. He tells everyone that the day he found you was the luckiest day of his life."

"Sabina." Impulsively Reuben covered her smooth small hand with his, for she was still absent-mindedly toying with the tiny thimble on the counter. He looked down into her sweet, earnest face, just as earnestly, himself. "That is not all of it. It is not luck

Sabina surprised Reuben by asking, "Reuben, do you ever pray?"

alone or even the hard, grueling work I have known that has brought this degree of success; it's more than that, but I can hardly explain it. It is something inside me. I have felt all along that in some way, somehow, I will win."

Then Sabina said a thing that Reuben dreaded for her to mention. She asked him about his religion. "Reuben, do you ever pray?" He was a little surprised at her asking him a question like that, for praying was a subject that people did not discuss very much. It was considered fanatical and a little embarrassing to mention things like that. Looking down into her face, he saw her reason for asking. She had heard some of the local talk about him, without a doubt. One parson openly called him an infidel; he had the name of being one who did not put too much stock in religion of any kind.

He did not answer her for a while, but just looked past her out of the many-paned windows of the store. Pa and Ma Conners had had them all washed and clean when he got back from his last trip. Across the dirt street several horses were tied in front of the blacksmith shop. Doc Boyd had just emerged from his high-stooped house and was climbing into his rig to go on some sick call. The whole town was buzzing and busy, and Reuben had helped to make it so, with his brains and brawn. Now, Sabina was touching on a tender spot—his relation to God and religion. He had been very bitter at the turn that life had taken for him. He had been sure—when he had lain starving, cold, sick, and miserable those horrible months in a military prison—that God had turned away His face from him and cared not a whit for him. But had He? Had He? Sabina had lost two brothers in the war, and still she trusted, and her mother, too.

"Sabina," he began, "you may not understand, but I—well—I somehow am afraid to trust my life again to God. My mother prayed continually for me. I prayed too—well, after I began to see the necessity of it—but look, did He hear? To me, it seemed as if we did not matter, and He had no time for such as we."

Sabina's hands trembled a little as she laced and relaced a bit of braid. It was plain by the look on her face that her faith in God had never wavered. "Let

53

me ask you something, Reuben," she said a little
hesitantly. "I don't mean to pry, but were you or even
your folks very religious before the war?"

"Never thought much of religion, then, I guess,"
he answered, lightly. "Even mother—oh, she was good
and kind and taught us our 'Now I lay me' and to be
true and honest, but we hardly ever were inside a
church, to my remembrance."

"Then how can you judge God on evidence like
that?" she asked reasonably enough. "How could you
be sure you were praying the right kind of prayers
and doing the things God wanted you to do?"

"Well, you have got me there," he laughed a little
ruefully. "I guess I did go to God only when I got
into a pinch, and things were going against me. But
look. What did it help you folks to pray? You lost
your home—all that you had. Si and George were
killed. What good did religion do you?"

Sabina smiled a little, and Reuben watching
thought there was never such a sweet and good girl
as she. "Reuben," she said, "if you do not have a real
working religion like mother and father brought us
children up to believe in with all our hearts, you

will hardly understand what I am going to tell you. It is like daddy says: you can't take any one thing and judge man or God by it."

"I think I can see the point you are making, Sabina. How can I expect God to jump and answer my prayers when I am frantic, when I have never let Him have any spot in my life when things were going along all right?"

"Well, that isn't exactly what I mean, but you are on the right track. You see, we all know that Jefferson Davis prayed. So did John Brown, and he thought he was led by God to strike at the institution of slavery in the bold way that he did. Abraham Lincoln was said to be a man of prayer. I believe God answers all prayers that are sincere in His way. And His way is not always our way."

Reuben's face was a study. "Yes, I see your point," he said slowly. "God does not always make it rosy for His followers; I can see that. For Jefferson Davis, a lost cause. John Brown, death by execution. For Lincoln, the assassin's bullet. And you really think God can bring His will out of even things like that?"

55

"Oh, yes, Reuben. If mother and father had not known Si and George were good and religious, I don't see how they could have borne the sorrow of their loss. But mother and father—yes, and I also—believe we will see them again. Did you ever read Lincoln's Second Inaugural, Reuben? It was written only a few days before he died. It was one of the most wonderful speeches I ever read."

"No, I don't believe I ever did, Sabina."

"You didn't? Oh, Reuben, it was so beautiful that I memorized the last part of it, and you can see that God was having His way in making this country a better place, even if it took a terrible war. Let me say it to you, and you will like it as well as I do."

"I'd like to hear it, Sabina."

"'Fondly do we hope—fervently do we pray—that this mighty scourge of war may speedily pass away. Yet, if God wills that it continue until all the wealth piled by the bondman's two hundred and fifty years of unrequited toil shall be sunk, and until every drop of blood drawn with the lash shall be paid by another drawn with the sword, as was said three thousand years ago, so still it must be said, "The judgments of the Lord are true and righteous altogether."

"'With malice toward none; with charity for all; with firmness in the right, as God gives us to see the right, let us strive on to finish the work we are in; to bind up the nation's wounds; to care for him who shall have borne the battle, and for his widow, and his orphan—to do all which may achieve and cherish a just and lasting peace among ourselves, and with all nations.'"

"A beautiful thing, Sabina," Reuben answered.

"It is, and I believe like father has often said, 'God looks down, and takes the hard things that wickedness brings on the earth, and does the best for us all that He can, as we let Him.' We can't see the end from the beginning and the whole picture of life as God can."

Customers began to come into the store, and the evening trade started, which cut in on their conversation. Sabina went home, and Reuben hustled around, all business, but he pondered what she had said. There was a reasonableness in it that he liked. And down in his heart, he was glad and proud that Sabina was a true and an earnest girl.

Reuben Takes a Bride

A MINISTER of the —— church had started some meetings in the schoolhouse, and Reuben determined to go and see whether he could straighten out his thoughts about God and heaven. He thought much on what Sabina had said about God and about prayer. Davis prayed. Yes, it had been told all through the South that he had prayed all night sometimes, yet the South was defeated. Everyone said that Lincoln had prayed. Why, he had read once that Lincoln had told Phillips Brooks, the great preacher, that he could not bear up under the burdens of life if it were not for prayer. Yet at the hour of receiving his greatest answer, he was struck down.

Reuben's mother prayed—she said she did in the letters she wrote. Reuben had prayed in the wet, stinking barracks, smelling of gaping, gangrenous wounds, and death—in the prison camp, when even sleep was an agony. Every time he went to sleep, he dreamed he was in the old plantation kitchen. Aunt Car'line was always making pone in those dreams. He'd see her lift the lid of the skillet, and there it lay —crusty and golden. She'd always shove a crock of soft, fresh butter toward him and would say in her soft drawl, "Dah, now, Reuben, honey, eat till yo' busts." But always as he reached for the knife to cut himself a huge crusty wedge to dredge with butter, he would awaken, in the horrors of near starvation hunger, in his filthy cell. His teeth loosened. His hair dropped out by the handfuls. His vision was seriously impaired. He had a constant raging headache. He knew he would have died, too, if the war had not ended when it did.

Going to church started Reuben to reading the Bible, and he got more interested than he had believed possible. He had never actually read the Bible; indeed he had not even owned one. But on his last trip to New York, he made it a point to go to a bookstore and buy himself a good copy of the Holy Scriptures. On the train while returning home, he read almost constantly in the New Testament, learning things he did not dream were there. He began, little by little, to make churchgoing a habit, even though he was a little self-conscious at first. Then, timidly, he began to try to pray in the solitude of his room. He thought afterward that God surely had to do a lot of piecing in to make anything of his early prayers. But they did his soul good, and he felt the blessing of God as he had never dreamed possible. And praying became easier for him.

When he told Sabina about it—it was so easy to talk to her—she seemed always to understand. He told her that at first he felt as he had felt as a child, when he tried to find his mother's room down the long hallway of his old home. He felt along the wall, examining every doorway until he came to one with a crack of light under the door. His mother always left a candle burning on an old bureau in her room. When he found the light, he always found mother— and comfort if he was sick or afraid.

It was on the way home from prayer meeting that Reuben asked Sabina to be his wife. He had pondered this move for a long time, but had delayed, for he had felt that he had so little to offer her. But now he had exciting news to add to the gladness of their new relationship, for he knew in his heart that Sabina would accept him. He felt sure that she loved him as he loved her.

The air was cool that night, and she wore a white woolen shawl. The stars shone so brightly that it seemed as if one could reach up and pick a few, like daisies from the bright meadows of heaven. They walked slowly, for the church was too close to Sabina's house to get much said, if they didn't. So Reuben told her of his and Pa Conners's new plan.

"We have decided to start up another store—over in Creek Center," he said, his voice full of emotion. "They are putting a spur of the railroad through there, and there isn't a store nearer than Millertown. He told me I could have *that* store. It is my chance—I mean our chance!"

"But who will help pa in the store here?" asked Sabina. "He needs someone who will take hold better than Chet Peters or any of the fellows who work around when things are busy. He is getting up in years."

"He looks and acts younger than he did when I came here seven years ago," Reuben told her. "I thought he and ma were old then, though actually they were only in their early fifties. But I guess trouble and sorrow do more to age a person than years do. I spoke to pa about your brother Bob. He may be young, but he is good, and I believe he will throw himself into it. He starts to work next Monday."

Reuben loved Sabina because her first thought in any good fortune was whether their pleasure was going to work a hardship on anyone else. She was to carry this trait of character, so self-abnegating, and so loving, all through a long and beautiful life.

"That is where we will work you into the picture, Sabina," Reuben told her proudly. "Pa knows how I feel about you, so we have decided this: I will do the buying for both stores, and you will keep the books for both of them. It will be just like a big city store!"

So did these two lay plans for a life that Reuben fondly hoped and believed would be devoid of the mistakes and pitfalls that plague others—a life that he believed would retrieve again a fortune that was lost, because it was not built on brains, only brawn. His own hands, hard and calloused now, had learned the secret and the pleasure of the cleansing value of hard work and the joy of real self-accomplishment.

Sabina prepared a hope chest, and her fine needlework was the envy of all the girls. Her mother, jealous of the privilege, made her dress. Remembering the days before the war, she wanted her only daughter to have white satin. But Sabina herself objected to that.

"It just isn't practical, Mother. You know I would never have another use for it, and it would lie in a box and get yellow and do no one any good."

"But, dear, you get married only once——"

"All the more reason to be realistic and practical, Mother. Let's send by Reuben for poplin, or taffeta, the next time he goes to New York——"

"Oh, Sabina," laughed her mother. "You haven't got a shred of romance about you. The idea. Letting

Reuben—of all people—select the cloth for your wedding dress!"

Sabina laughed at that, but she still held to her point. "He can get a better buy than we can, and get a better selection. Anyway, he won't get to see it until it is made. You can't tell a thing about cloth until it's made up."

So Reuben, secretly pleased, was given the unusual responsibility of picking out those fourteen yards of blue taffeta Sabina wanted for her bridal dress.

On the same trip he found a small tailoring shop down in lower Manhattan and had a fine suit made for himself. A Prince Albert, they called it, and it was resplendent with black satin lapels and buttons covered with the same gleaming material.

At last the day of all days arrived. They were married in the parlor of the Seymour home, which was resplendently decorated with "pineys" and roses and flags, as the tall irises used to be called. The room, very large and dignified with furniture Corbin had made, was filled with guests. Everyone in town came, and a few from the countryside. Sabina was

5   Reuben waited at the foot of the stairs for Sabina and her father.

a great favorite, with her music and her teaching and her general sweet way she had with everyone.

Her dress had hoops, naturally, for everyone wore hoops for special occasions if they had them. If they didn't, they scraped potatoes and made homemade starch of such great stiffness as to comfort the heart of the hoopless, so the wearer was not altogether hopeless.

Her dress had a shapely tight little basque that showed up the tininess of her waist. "So small that Reuben can span it with his two hands," Ma Seymour had bragged. The huge sleeves pleated at the shoulders, and ending with a tight-fitting sleeve over the forearm, edged with white ruching, Reuben said came from Paris. Dozens of tiny gold buttons wandered down the tight basque and up her tight sleeves. A lovely, lovely bride, everyone said. And Reuben, tall and blond, waiting at the stairs for Sabina and her father to make the grand descent, was a fine figure himself, and stirred the heart of every maiden in the room.

Sabina's wedding cake was a miracle of beauty, and the flavor was not one whit behind. The recipe

—or receipt, as it was called—started something like this:

> Take the finest and nicest flour, 5 lbs.; very nice butter, 3 lbs.; English currants, nicely washed, dried, and dredged, 5 lbs.; sifted loaf sugar, 2 lbs.; nice sweet almonds, blanched, 1 lb.; nutmegs, 2; mace, 4 oz.; cloves, ¼ oz.; lemon and orange peel, each ½ lb.; grape wine, 1 pt.; eggs, 16.
> Bake in a medium hot oven for four hours, and be sure to cover with brown paper while baking.

Everyone agreed that the marriage was the greatest event the little town of Conners had witnessed. And Pa and Ma Conners were just as proud of Reuben as if it were their very own son who had taken unto himself a wife. It hardly seemed possible that he was not their own, instead of a homesick and homeless soldier who had adopted them as much as they had adopted him. They told each other several times that evening that he was the handsomest fellow there.

There had been enough money to furnish the house that they were to live in at Creek Center. Reuben had Corbin making things for a full year before the wedding. The house was only a cottage —four rooms down and two up—and partially damaged when the armies of both sides took their toll of property as they marched back and forth. But it is amazing what a few bags of plaster, several buckets of paint, and a few rolls of wallpaper can do to completely transform a place.

Sabina's mother, a born manager, saw to it that there were sheets, feather beds, pillow cases, and fat pillows enough for an army, to say nothing of table-cloths, towels, and crisp curtains.

As used to be the custom, the kitchen was not in the house proper. It was off a few feet behind the main house. This was fine in hot weather, for the heat of the stove did not affect the whole house. But in rainy and cold weather, it had its weak points. Reuben installed a Farmer's Favorite stove and hired Aunt Zinnia, a good-natured colored woman, and known to be a fine cook, to have charge. For the rental of a good, roomy cabin and all the wood they needed, plus milk and butter and a weekly stipend, Uncle Zack, her husband, agreed to be the handy man about the place. He proved to be exceedingly handy, too; his willing services included care of the horse and the two cows and helping in the store in a pinch. He also took care of the flower beds and such of the vegetable garden that Aunt Zinnia did not claim as a part of her domain.

The new stove remained pretty new so far as Aunt Zinnia was concerned. She used it reluctantly, even suspiciously on occasions, but there were some things that always would taste better cooked in an old brick oven or over the fireplace in a big black iron pot. She was more at home turning out puddings, cakes, hominy, roasts, stews, and hot breads when she labored among the more familiar trivits, spits, irons, long-legged skillets, pots, and Dutch oven. But she often set a bouquet of flowers on top of the stove and acted grandiose and proud of it if visitors from among her friends happened to step into the kitchen.

Business thrived at the store in Creek Center. Reuben often told Sabina that they were well on the way toward building the fortune that he had dreamed of during the terrible days that followed the war.

"My portion!" he would laugh, looking at the wide aisles and the full shelves. But there was one nagging little hitch that worried Reuben a little, though he was ashamed to admit it. The store actually belonged to Pa Conners. Every time Reuben would suggest buying it, the older man would laugh and say, "Why should you, Reuben? You helped me to amass all this. It will all be yours when ma and I are through with it. Keep your money and save all you want to after the bills are paid."

In spite of everything, Reuben wondered if pa had made a will, or if he thought it was not necessary. He knew he should say something to Pa Conners about it, for though he and ma were in fine health, they might not have thought of all the ramifications of the thing. For after all, Reuben was not a legal heir, and any cousin or nephew could step in with more legal rights than Reuben, who had given years of his life to make all this possible. Alger could. Reuben knew that right well, and he knew that Alger would if he got half a chance.

When he said something to Sabina about it, she laughed away his fears. "You would *really* sound like a loving son if you began to urge pa and ma to make wills, wouldn't you, Reuben? Well, don't worry. They are only in their sixties, and pa looks younger than when I first saw him ten years ago."

"Well, I'm not going to worry. Pa knows business and life, and he will have taken care of my rights in this. Of that I am sure." This was from Reuben, who was going to build so sure, and so true that nothing would tear the structure of his life away. He was going to be sure of his "portion."

A Book Agent Comes to Town

IN THE YEARS that followed, Sabina bloomed with the beauty and sweetness of maturity and motherhood. Four little boys and two dainty girls filled Sabina's hours with sewing and mending, music and homemaking. The cottage grew with the family. Reuben had added and enlarged until the original shape of the honeymoon cottage was almost forgotten.

Their oldest son was named Reuben—"after his pa," Aunt Zinnia proudly told everyone. "An' ain't he the very 'spit' of him?" she would declare. "Frangy, feisty, and unpredictable!" Reuben did not like this summary of his character by outspoken Aunt Zinnia. It smacked too much of grandpa's dark predictions: "Unstable as water, thou shalt not excel." But Reuben said nothing—only went on, working harder than ever.

The other three boys were after the same pattern: Joseph, Benjamin, and Ephraim. The two little girls were Rose and Lily. "You sure do beat all, Reuben," laughed Sabina after Lily, the youngest, was born. "Our boys are all saddled with Bible names, but our girls could not be Hulda, or Rachel, or Rebekah, no. They both have to be flowers to please their father."

"They are flowers," Reuben asserted stoutly, looking down into Lily's little red face—"both of them."

"She doesn't look much like a lily to me," Sabina remarked realistically. "You should have named her Balsam, from the way she keeps us up nights, or Scarlet Sage, from the way she looks."

"Sabina!" Reuben looked horrified. "And you're her mother, too! Why, she's a beautiful baby! Beautiful!"

They were pretty little girls, and the boys were sturdy and wholesome. Both parents saw to it that they were well behaved and good, nor was the spiritual side of their lives neglected. Every Sunday the

"Does the Bible tell anything about the end of the world?"

family was in church, unless illness, inclement weather, or a combination of both prevented.

Pa Conners was in his early seventies, but hale and hearty and did more work than he was able to do fifteen years before when Reuben came upon him weakly edging a barrel of ill-favored sweet potatoes into the shambles of a ruined store. Happiness and the smile of good fortune do a great deal more for health than most people like to admit.

Reuben, Joseph, and Benjamin were all in school when the old book agent came to the village. He did not come to Pelman's store, or if he did, he came when Reuben was out, and he missed him. But Reuben heard of him the next day. Old man Bankhead had ordered one of the books, and he told Reuben about it in the store the next day. He said it would be a month or two before the fellow said he'd deliver it, but it was a book that looked "powerful interestin'. It explains what the Bible says about the end of the world." Instantly Reuben was all attention. He turned to the old man in amazement. "Does the Bible tell anything about the end of the world?" he asked incredulously.

"It shore does," the old man asserted, proud to be the purveyor of important and breath-taking information. "That feller, he read lots of passages to me, and it fair gave me the creeps. I been goin' to church fer nigh onto sixty years, and no preacher ever said anything about the world comin' to an end."

"Well, you bring that book, and let me see it, when it's delivered," Reuben told him. "And tell the agent to come and spin his yarn to me. He might make another sale."

"I shore will, Reuben." Old man Bankhead went away, proud of the sensation he had caused. He waited impatiently for a book that would not only threaten Reuben's portion, but would show him that there is only one sure foundation, and that any other is building upon the sand.

The cold fall rains had begun when old Mr. Bankhead appeared one afternoon dripping but jubilant and happy, with a small black book carefully wrapped up in an old coat. "I didn't get no chance to tell him you wanted one," he told Reuben cheerfully. "He came while I was out to the woods lot gettin' a wagonload of wood, and ma paid him and

76

he went on. I told ma that the money was in the big sugar bowl up on top the dresser by the fireplace, and I told her to tell him you wanted to see him, but she clean fergot."

He held his small copy of *Thoughts on Daniel and Revelation* out for Reuben to see. "You kin borry mine any time you're a mind to," he offered.

"*Thoughts, Critical and Practical, on the Books of Daniel and the Revelation*," read Reuben. "Why, Sir," he said in a puzzled tone, looking up at old man Bankhead, "you have got yourself gypped. No one can understand Daniel or Revelation. They told us so up at the church. They told me they are written about old people and old nations and cities all done and gone long ago. They do not apply today."

"That ain't what the feller told me," the old man protested, his blue eyes shining with the warm zeal of the interpreter. "He said Dan'l and Revelations is fer us t'day, and they tell us all about things we ort t' know. I tell you what—you read this here book, Reuben, and kinder explain it t' me as y' go along. I ain't had the chanct at eddication 't you had. Do it fer an old man, Reub."

77

Any objections he might have raised were stilled as he looked into the eager, quivering face of the old man. It took so little to mean so much. Mr. Bankhead had a fine mind, but as he said, he had never had a chance at schooling. Folks told it around, though, that he got himself a primer and learned to read while he plowed the swampland on his father's farm. He was always inventing things and new ways of doing things. They all laughed at a fan he rigged up to fan himself while riding in the heat in the old rig he had. It was fastened to the axle and was really ingenious. But Reuben did not laugh. "I call that pretty clever," he told Mr. Bankhead.

So Reuben promised to read the new book through to him, explaining it as he went, as well as he could. Reuben told Sabina afterward that he did it to please the old fellow more than anything else.

"He hasn't got much to be glad for, Sabina, with that wasp-tongued wife of his. Folks say he has to take off his shoes and shake his coat in the entry before she will let him into that spotless living room of hers."

"That's good of you to read to him," Sabina answered as she deftly set a patch on the seat of Ephraim's little pants. "I do declare, Reuben, this boy is the hardest on clothes of any child I ever saw—worse than all the other children put together."

"Must take after me," Reuben commented, grinning. "I remember mother complaining about how hard I was on my clothes."

And that's how it came about that Reuben started reading a little black book about two mysterious books in the Bible to an old neighbor man. They set the time for the middle of the afternoon, when there was usually a lull in the store.

Reading *Thoughts, Critical and Practical, on the Book of Daniel* was started blithely enough one bright fall day, at the back part of the store. There was an old rocker and a straight chair by Reuben's desk. He gave Mr. Bankhead the chair, and the old man sat down all relaxed to give himself over to the deep pleasure of the occasion.

Fortunately nobody came into the store, and Reuben was able to go all the way through chapter one and to read aloud the chapter from the Bible to him beside. It was amazingly clear and not hard to understand in the least. Reuben told Sabina about it afterward. When he came in from the store to eat supper, she looked up from ladling rich potato soup into the soup plates to smile at him. Aunt Zinnia came in with a great platter of corn bread, which she'd have them know she didn't bake in that new-fangled stove contraption. She baked it right on the hearth in a good iron skillet just like the Lord intended. "How did you and Mr. Bankhead get along with that book?" Sabina asked pleasantly.

Instead of answering, Reuben asked her a question. "Sabina, do you know where our Rollin's *Ancient History* is? I got into some stuff today that I'd like to verify."

After supper was eaten, while Sabina was busying herself with the children and Aunt Zinnia was capably cleaning up the supper table, Reuben opened Rollin's *History*. When things got quiet and young Reuben and Joseph were working hard at their homework by the dining table, Sabina sat down with her everlasting mending.

"That first chapter in Mr. Bankhead's book was as clear as crystal, Sabina. I don't see why so many ministers are afraid of the Book of Daniel. If it keeps up like it starts, a baby could understand."

"What's it about, Reuben?" Sabina asked.

"I asked Mr. Bankhead if I could keep it and read it to you tonight, but he wanted to take it home and explain it to his wife. He is all worked up and excited about it. But I think I can remember enough to get it across if you will get the Bible. My lap is full of these history books."

Sabina handed him the big Bible he had bought several years before at a bookstore on one of his trips to New York.

"The first chapter of Daniel, as I see it and as it was explained, has to do with the captives the king of Babylon took when he overthrew the city of Jerusalem. He took some of the royal house into his palace to train them to be wise men. There; read it, Sabina. The first chapter and the third to the sixth verses."

Sabina pulled the elegant parlor lamp a little nearer and read aloud, in her warm expressive voice:

6   81

" 'And the king spake unto Ashpenaz the master of his eunuchs, that he should bring certain of the children of Israel, and of the king's seed, and of the princes; children in whom was no blemish, but well favoured, and skilful in all wisdom, and cunning in knowledge, and understanding science, and such as had ability in them to stand in the king's palace, and whom they might teach the learning and the tongue of the Chaldeans. And the king appointed them a daily provision of the king's meat, and of the wine which he drank: so nourishing them three years, that at the end thereof they might stand before the king. Now among these were of the children of Judah, Daniel, Hananiah, Mishael, and Azariah.' "

"You see, Sabina, the conflict, or rather the story, began when these fellows refused to eat the food that the king wanted them to eat, and made an issue of it. In those days it was a pretty serious thing to buck up against a king. They had power to kill one at the drop of a hat, it seems."

"You don't have to go back that far to find some pretty mean ways by the kings," Sabina observed. "As I remember it, Henry the Eighth was pretty much of a fellow to get rid of anyone who displeased him. And Bloody Mary, his daughter, killed people —good people, too—right and left."

Reuben looked at his wife appreciatively. It went through his mind what a queen among women she was and how lucky he was to have her. Most women would not know that those old kings even existed, much less be able to converse intelligently about them.

"Well, it seems that the Jews are careful about what they eat. A good Jew—I mean an orthodox Jew—will die rather than touch unclean meat, so these young princes decided not to eat the food the king provided for them."

"Oh, I know," Sabina contributed. "Jews—good ones, I mean—won't eat pork. And they won't have anything to do with lard. And there are some kinds of fowls they won't eat—ducks, I think, and geese—and some kinds of fish. There must be some reason behind it, but I never found out why."

"Well, I found out some of the reasons today. There are places in the Old Testament where pork and other unclean things are forbidden. Daniel asked that fellow Ashpenaz—I think his name was—to give him and his companions 'pulse' to eat and water to drink. I remember the man Uriah Smith, who wrote the book, said that the Hebrew word *zeroim* is translated pulse. It means 'herbs bearing seed or fruits

83

bearing seed.' What Daniel asked for was a vegetarian diet—one made up of cereals, legumes, fruits, nuts, and vegetables."

"Why, could they be healthy on a diet like that?"

"Well, Ashpenaz was afraid they would not be, and dared not let them do it, till Daniel asked him to try them out for—let's see; oh, here it is—ten days. Read what happened at the end of ten days. Or first, listen to what he said to Daniel: 'And the prince of the eunuchs said unto Daniel, I fear my lord the king, who hath appointed your meat and your drink: for why should he see your faces worse liking than the children which are of your sort? then shall ye make me endanger my head to the king.' Read the fifteenth and sixteenth verses, Sabina."

> " 'And at the end of ten days their countenances appeared fairer and fatter in flesh than all the children which did eat the portion of the king's meat. Thus Melzar took away the portion of their meat, and the wine that they should drink; and gave them pulse.' "

"You know, Sabina, what you said about people not being healthy on just a vegetable diet sort of interested me, for another soldier and I lived on just vegetables for a long time during the war and were glad to get them. For eight or nine weeks we were hiding out and were cut off from the rest of the division we were in. There was a farm garden right near that we lived on. There were wild grapes in the woods and pumpkins, onions, and a few ears of corn. Oh, yes, a few turnips, and once in a while a beet."

"How did you make out?" Sabina asked.

"I tell you, it was funny," Reuben said. "We both felt fine, but laid it to the fact that we had good, strong constitutions. But I wouldn't be surprised if there was not more to it than that."

"I did hear once—I don't know where I read it —that Benjamin Franklin was one of these people."

"Vegetarians?" queried Reuben.

"I guess that's what they call it. In the article I read, the author expressed amazement that a man of such tremendous brain energy could subsist on an all-vegetable diet."

At the beginning the reading of the book went off fine. Then for several days they were prevented from reading another chapter. Reuben had to go on the road, buying up wool and taking calves and sheep to the railroad center. On an impulse of his own—since Thanksgiving and Christmas were so near—he picked up geese and turkeys in trade for goods every chance he got. At Sabina's suggestion, he got Corbin to help him fit up a large wagon with shelves, fitting it up like a small store on wheels. One week out of the month he was out with the wagon, until they found an old man to take over who was capable of handling it. Reuben was glad to be back at his old duties again.

It was as he told Sabina: he had too many irons in the fire to take care of them all. He was not a little amused at old man Bankhead. He no sooner drove his huckster wagon in than there he stood in front of the store with the ubiquitous black book in his hands. Reuben felt so sorry for the old fellow, that he told him to slip over that evening after supper, and he and Sabina both would help him with the second chapter. And that was the chapter that got the whole household stirred up.

A Book That Stirred the Family

SUPPER was over, the three younger children were in bed, and Aunt Zinnia had cleared up and made her way across the yard to the ample cabin where she and Uncle Zack lived. Young Reuben and Benjamin were sitting at the dining table wrestling with the next day's studies. Mr. Bankhead sat down in the Sleepy Hollow rocker near to the fireplace and put his old hat under the chair on the floor. Sabina took the Bible and read the chapter through first, as they had all agreed was best.

It was the first time any one of those sitting there had ever read of the mighty king of Babylon and of his memorable dream. It seemed that he had had the dream and the next morning could not remem-

87

ber what he had dreamed about. And the more he tried to think and call it to mind, the more exasperated he became.

"I've done that," remarked Reuben. "Dreamed something, but had only a hazy, aggravating memory of it the next morning."

"Yes, but you did not have any magicians and wise men to fall back on," laughed Sabina.

"Nor had the power of life and death over folks," added Mr. Bankhead importantly.

"That must have been pretty hard on the wise men, to have the king demand of them to tell him a dream he couldn't remember himself," Sabina said reflectively.

"The way I see it, they had made great claims of being able even to read the thoughts, and I guess old King Nebuchadnezzar was catching up with them. Read again what he said to them, Sabina. He was a pretty wise old fellow."

"That was after they had told the king that they would be glad to interpret the dream if he would only tell it to them," Sabina answered, running her finger down the page trying to find the passage.

"Yes, Mother," young Reuben said, looking up from his geography book, "and I liked where they said there wasn't a king anywhere who would ask such a thing of their wise men." They all laughed at that, for it was clear that the boys were getting as much Bible as they were arithmetic and geography.

"It won't hurt them any," Reuben said. "Let them listen. Bible won't hurt anyone!"

"I found that verse," Sabina said. "It is in the eighth verse—I mean it begins there. 'The king answered and said, I know of a certainty that ye would gain the time, because ye see the thing is gone from me. But if ye will not make known unto me the dream, there is but one decree for you: for ye have prepared lying and corrupt words to speak before me, till the time be changed: therefore tell me the dream, and I shall know that ye can shew me the interpretation thereof.' "

When they started into the explanation from the book, the boys frankly stopped studying and pulled their chairs up into the circle. All could see the scene as it took place so many centuries ago: the angry king, the terrified and protesting wise men, at last condemned to death; then, when the soldiery came around to slay even the student wise men—Daniel and the other three along with the rest—they ran up against something they had not expected. Daniel, after finding out the reason, asked the king why he was in such a hurry to kill all the wise men.

"I suppose the king figured that if the old wise men were up a stump, the young ones would be as bad off as the old ones—or even worse," Joseph remarked.

They all marveled at the lad who sought the Lord in prayer and to whom the Lord revealed the dream. They pictured the king sitting there on his throne and listening with delight as the Hebrew captive lad told him with such great confidence the dream that he had dreamed. He did not ask the king if that was what he dreamed; he said, "Thou, O king, sawest, and behold a great image."

Old man Bankhead was speechless with delight at the furor that he was causing. He just sat back, his pleased and gentle old eyes resting first on one face and then on another, as the discussion got more heated and interesting.

The great golden image of the dream came in for a little discussion before they went forward with the interpretation. The great image of the king's dream, with its head of gold, its breast and arms of silver, its sides of brass, its legs and feet of iron, represented the history of the world, beginning with the golden age of Babylon.

"Let's hear again what that young feller told the king; then you tell me what it all means, Reuben," Mr. Bankhead said.

"I'll just read what the Bible says right here," Reuben answered. "I'll tell you, it's as plain as the nose on your face." And he took the Bible and read aloud:

> "'After thee shall arise another kingdom [Medo-Persia] inferior to thee, and another third kingdom of brass ["That was Greece," Reuben inserted, in an aside], which shall bear rule over all the earth. And the fourth kingdom shall be strong as iron ["Rome, of course"].'"

"Say, Reuben, that puts us down in the feet, don't it?" queried Mr. Bankhead. "I heard my old mother say one time that some fellers once preached that the Lord is coming in clouds. Do you figger that

—well—we could be gettin' nigh t' somethin' like that?"

"I don't know for sure, Mr. Bankhead," replied Reuben, "but it kind of looks like it. Look what it says: 'In the days of these kings shall the God of heaven set up a kingdom, which shall never be destroyed.'"

"That must have been the stone that was cut out without hands, Reuben. Where was that?" Sabina asked. She had stopped her sewing and was looking up texts in a huge old family Bible that her mother had given her. "Here it is," she said.

> "'Thou sawest till that a stone was cut out without hands, which smote the image upon his feet that were of iron and clay, and brake them to pieces. Then was the iron, the clay, the brass, the silver, and the gold, broken to pieces together, and became like the chaff of the summer threshingfloors; and the wind carried them away, that no place was found for them: and the stone that smote the image became a great mountain, and filled the whole earth.'"

Reuben laid the book in Mr. Bankhead's trembling old hands. "You know, Mr. Bankhead, I had no idea you had a book that would make those old books so real. Why, if it makes the rest of that old dead book as clear as this chapter, I'd surely like to have one myself. If that old bookseller comes back, tell him there is another sale."

"He told me that the books of Dan'l and the Revelation ain't no more dead than I am. And I'll sure tell him if I see him. But Reuben, you won't quit studying with me, will you? I don't know when I ever had such a nice time. Folks ain't got time fer old folks, nowadays, it seems like."

"Oh, no, we'll go through this book together," Reuben promised. "But this chapter astonishes me. If I did not believe in the Bible, it would set me right, for that book had to be written by a higher power than man. It covers twenty-five centuries at the very least in one stroke. Why, I know all about the four kingdoms here. I've studied them. It could not be put more compact, nor more accurately. Come back tomorrow, Mr. Bankhead, and we'll see what the man Uriah Smith has to say about chapter three."

The old man was overjoyed that he was causing such a to-do, and he smiled most of the time now. The reading of the book ceased to be a neighborly act, for the Pelman family became honestly and excitedly interested in what they read. Whether they would have gone on if they could have seen into the future is a matter of guesswork. But fortunately for us all, we cannot see the sunshine, nor yet the shadows that will beset our way.

Reuben never went halfway about anything. Every time he thought to challenge the author, he went quickly to his well-stocked bookcases and checked with musty old tomes he had collected with so much love and care. Since he had established a home, he haunted the old bookstores every time he went to New York to buy. Bagster, Josephus, Gibbon, Rollin, D'Aubigné—these were a few of the authors he liked. Sabina never saw him so exercised over anything like this, however. The colporteur never returned, so Reuben finally dispatched a letter to the press in Battle Creek, so he could have a book of his own. Mr. Bankhead could never be persuaded to leave his copy.

"I can't make it out, Sabina," Reuben said one night after the old man had gone home. "That book tallies right with history, yet it is the strangest teaching I ever heard. I never heard of some of the stuff he tells in the book, yet there are the proofs right there in the Bible—in the New Testament, too. Take that chapter we read some from tonight, Matthew 24; why, Sabina, the Lord *must* be going to come, well, fairly soon, and I can't see that the people know a thing about it."

"The preaching of the coming of the Lord is not a new thing," Sabina observed thoughtfully. "You know Grandmother Milbank came from New Hampshire, and I have heard her and mother both talk about what they called the Millerite movement. It was in the thirties and forties, as I remember."

"Say, didn't they have some kind of prediction that did not come true? It seems like I have heard something about that. My sister that died was born the very year. Let's see, it was 1844."

"Yes, Reuben," Sabina said. "Grandmother said that they thought the Lord was going to come that year, but He did not come, and the movement went to pieces, I guess."

"Well, all I have to say is that this book couldn't have been written by any bunch of fanatics, for the whole thing is historically sound. I've checked on it at every step."

Reuben sat for a while in Sabina's fancy rocker and pondered, gazing unseeingly at her pretty Brussels carpet that was her pride and joy. Then he jumped up.

"Well, this won't buy the baby a new dress," he laughed, rubbing Lily's fuzzy head with his big hands. She crowed with delight and seized his big thumb in her dimpled fingers.

"Nor pay for the one she's got," Sabina added laughingly as he left to go and see how the after-supper business was doing at the store. The hour was nine. Sabina hustled the older boys to bed and went to see to the kitchen fire and the laying out of supplies for Aunt Zinnia for breakfast.

Reuben had built a veranda to the outdoor kitchen, but Sabina always lit a lamp and set it in the window and carried a lantern. She almost stepped on a big black snake once and was wary of them ever since.

Aunt Zinnia had set the batter for buckwheat cakes that Reuben and the boys thought they could never get along without. Sabina saw with some amusement that Aunt Zinnia had cooked the whole supper on the fireplace, disregarding with scorn the fine stove that Reuben had set up in the kitchen. The batter was set in a huge blue bowl and covered with a snowy fringed tea towel. Aunt Zinnia could not read a word, but Sabina knew she made her choice dishes by set measures that she murmured to herself as she made them. These cakes she knew would be the same always, for she never varied her way of making them: Six coffee cups of warm water and a dash of salt. A half cup of yeast out of the yeast jug, ready always for bread, crullers, buns, or buckwheat cakes. Then, buckwheat flour, enough to make a batter. That was what was getting bubbly right now in the big blue bowl.

The kitchen was in perfect order and clean as a pin. Sabina, her housewifely heart satisfied, returned to the house. Reuben came in, and they locked the house and retired for the night.

The more Reuben read in the book, the more exercised he became, for the truth of the coming of the Lord grew increasingly evident. He searched his

Bible for references on that event. He saw that at every turn the subject was mentioned. It was taught from the stone that smote the image on the feet to the king of the north mentioned in the eleventh chapter of Daniel. The first verse in the twelfth chapter troubled Reuben not a little. He read it to Sabina one night:

> "'And at that time shall Michael stand up, the great prince which standeth for the children of thy people: and there shall be a time of trouble, such as never was since there was a nation even to that same time: and at that time thy people shall be delivered, every one that shall be found written in the book. And many of them that sleep in the dust of the earth shall awake, some to everlasting life, and some to shame and everlasting contempt.'

"It says that there would be a time of trouble worse than any other time. Well, if I'd read this while I was in the prison camp, I'd have thought *it* was worse than any other time; but now since it is past, I know it was as Sherman himself said: that war is hell. It wasn't any worse than the Napoleonic Wars, the Wars of the Roses, or the suffering in the Crimean War only a few years ago. We have not seen that time of trouble yet."

"Our book came today," said Reuben.

"I think you're right, Reuben," Sabina answered. "But what does that mean about Michael standing up? I had to go see about the baby when you were reading that part. I'll be glad when our own book comes."

"Our book *has* come, my lady," Reuben laughed. "It came today. And I will read to you just what it says about that very thing." And Reuben swiftly leafed through the volume to find what he wanted to read. Then leaning back, so that the mellow light from the lamp fell on the white page, he read:

> "'We now come to the second question, What is the standing up of Michael? The key to the interpretation of this expression is furnished us in verses 2 and 3 of chapter 11: "There shall stand up yet three kings in Persia;" "A mighty king shall stand up, that shall rule with great dominion." There can be no doubt as to the meaning of these expressions in these instances. They signify to take the kingdom, to reign. The same expression in the verse under consideration must mean the same. At that time, Michael shall stand up, shall take the kingdom, shall begin to reign.'"

"Isn't Christ—you told me that Michael is just another name for Christ—isn't he reigning now, anyway?" Sabina asked.

"I guess He must be," Reuben answered slowly. "But as I see it, this reign He begins at His second coming is the promised throne of His father David. Look, it says at the bottom of the page to look at Luke 1:32, 33."

"I'll read that," Sabina answered. "Luke is the second or third book in the New Testament, isn't it?" she asked, leafing through the big Bible.

"Yes. Remember the old prayer we used to pray —or maybe you didn't as I did—'Matthew, Mark; Luke, and John, bless this bed I rest upon'? I don't much like that prayer, for I never did like praying to the saints; but it made me remember the order of the books at least. Have you found it?"

"I take it this was something someone said about Jesus when He was a small baby—no, it was what the angel said to Mary before He was born. Here it is: 'He shall be great, and shall be called the Son of the Highest: and the Lord God shall give unto him the throne of his father David: and he shall reign over the house of Jacob for ever; and of his kingdom there shall be no end.' Well, that nails it down. But some of the things there have not taken place yet. So we are not as close to the coming as it seemed at first."

"I don't know," Reuben said. "But I do know that some of the things we have been taking for granted can't be true. Now take this resurrection, for instance. If, as you and I have been taught all our lives, the good go to heaven when they die, and the bad folks go to burn in hell, what is the use of the resurrection? It doesn't make sense to me. There is something wrong somewhere."

"I've heard of the resurrection and I wondered about that lots of times," Sabina answered.

"So have I, and that is one of the reasons I had so little use for the Bible. I figured it did not make sense. But it says here in this book that the resurrection that will take place when Michael comes into His kingdom is not the regular resurrection but sort of a special one, just before the coming of the Lord and the regular resurrection. That knocks the idea that we go to our reward at death into a cocked hat."

"Do you remember that old circuit rider that used to come around here and preach from his 'brimstone wallet' as Aunt Zinnia said?"

"Yes, I do," Reuben answered slowly. "He was always shouting about standing before the Judge of all the universe and giving an account for all the sins we have committed. Well, I asked him one day when that judgment would be, and he all but took my head off and accused me of being a Christless infidel on the brink of perdition."

Sabina laughed. "I always wanted to ask him some things, myself. But he didn't seem to know very much but the hell-fire doctrine. Dad said one night after we got home that he could not reconcile the things Parson Bentt said with what he read in the Scriptures about God being just and merciful. Mother didn't like it, but dad always called him old Hell-Bentt. He wouldn't go if he knew ahead of time that he was going to preach, but he sometimes got caught."

They both laughed at that.

"Well, anyway," Reuben resumed, "I for one am glad that the old doctrine of going to heaven or hell at death is not so. It sort of put God into a tyrant category with me—sending a fellow up without a trial or anything."

The winter progressed with a few snowstorms and continued prosperity on the part of the Pelmans. They were concerned once about Pa Conners. He got pneumonia, and Reuben had to stay at the other store for several days. Sabina ably managed their store, though it was a strain.

When Reuben finally got home to stay—his visits before, during pa's illness, were always rushed—he had big news for the family. In fact he always had news, for he was ever eager to see how the world was progressing. When Sabina lit the kerosene lamps that night—and proud she was of them, too, for most of the neighbors still had candles—he said, "Well, Sabina, you can't guess what I saw when I was in New York this past week. I saw a light on display they call the Edison Incandescent. It was lighted by electricity. It was wonderful. Maybe you and I will yet see more wonderful things than that before we die."

"I think it would be a big time saver, to have light without having to fill lamps and wash chimneys all the time. I hear they have gas lights in New York. Did you see any, Reuben?"

"Oh, yes, I see them all the time. There are wonderful chandeliers in the president's house in Washington, where gas is used. They have a special fellow hired to light and to turn off the gas all over the place."

"I'd be a little afraid of gas, I believe," Sabina observed.

"That doesn't sound like you, Sabina," Reuben laughed. "Aunt Zinnia was afraid of the cooking stove. Your mother was wary of the sewing machine I got for you that Mr. Isaac Singer perfected and made so handy. You know, you can make things ever so much quicker than you used to."

"Yes, and they are a lot stronger, too. Mother would hardly believe that I finished a ruffled shirt for you and did all my other work in less than two days. It would not surprise me if they might try to do something about washing clothes one of these days."

"Especially if this new thing, electricity, comes into general use. They say it has wonderful powers. But that reminds me. You know that book *Thoughts, Critical, and Practical?*"

"On the Book of Daniel?" queried Sabina.

"Yes," Reuben answered. "There is one text in that last chapter of Daniel that tells about knowledge being increased and men running to and fro. Well, they are building a bridge over the East River from Manhattan to Brooklyn."

"No! How can they, Reuben? Why, that is a long way. Did you see it?"

"Well, it is a sight to behold. They have a kind of catwalk—just planks laid on top of the cables so the workmen could go across. Lots of people have wanted to go across, but very few go all the way. It is pretty scary away up there above the water. The day I walked across, I saw several men get out a little way, lose their nerve, and actually crawl back on their hands and knees. The crowd laughed at them, but there were few of the crowd who would do any better if they were up there."

The president who was in the White House that year (1881) was James Garfield. Reuben was fortunate enough to get to hear his inaugural address when he was in Washington, coming through from his trip to New York, following Pa Conners's illness. Garfield's mother was the first mother of a president to hear her son give the inaugural address. Reuben was touched by the fact that as soon as President Garfield pressed his lips to the Holy Bible, taking the oath of office, he turned to kiss his mother. He told someone later—and Reuben read it—that he did that because her heroic sacrifices, during long years of adversity and hardship, made that glad moment possible.

Reuben told Sabina of the wonderful elevated trains that had been started in New York. And at one place they had built a big house, big enough to hold several families. They called it Stuyvesant House, he told her.

"I wouldn't like that," Sabina replied. "Everybody's food smells, and children and garbage——"

"Yes, and they have to walk quite a way to get water, though I see carts selling water by the hogshead down in the streets. They get it from a good well they call the 'tea well.' I drank from that well the day I went to Barnum's Museum. I'll tell you, Sabina, knowledge *is* increasing, and it would not surprise me to find out that we are nearer to the coming of the Lord than either one of us realizes."

Sad as Aunt Zinnia was, it made her proud to see the pains
her "people were takin' fer Zack."

A Day to Consider

THE VERY MONTH that the news was telegraphed all over the country (by means of the wonderful new magnetic telegraph) that Pres. James Garfield was shot and lying at the point of death, old Uncle Zack died. Reuben had Corbin make a good coffin for him out of some walnut boards he had in the barn for which he had traded the year before. Sad as Aunt Zinnia was, it made her very proud to see the pains her "people were takin' fer Zack." Reuben put bright hinges and a good brass catch on the lid. Sabina lined it with muslin, and made a pillow for old Zack's head. The colored preacher preached Uncle Zack straight to heaven. When they got home from the funeral, Aunt Zinnia insisted on working as usual.

109

" 'Taint gonna hu't me any," she told them; "an' it 'pears like I'll feel ever s' much better if I jes' go on with my wo'k."

Then Aunt Zinnia hesitated and looked at Sabina. "I knowed well as you do when that preacher was a preachin' that Zack ain't in hebben. I heard you and Mister talkin'. Zack he's jes' layin' dar restin'. He lay dar an' res' till Gabriel blows de ho'n."

"Why, you are right, Zinnia!" Reuben said, filled with wonder. He told Sabina afterward that if Aunt Zinnia could catch truth so quickly while she was running to and fro readying up the house, cleaning vegetables, and making bread, anyone could understand who had a mind to. But neither one of them talked very much about another thing that was looming up in their studies.

One night Reuben mentioned it. "You know, Sabina," he said. "I can't get it off my mind what I read in that book about times and laws. You know—that power in Daniel 7 that would change times and laws?"

"Oh, yes. I think that Daniel 7 is a kind of repeat of Daniel 2, which tells of the four kingdoms

—Babylon, Medo-Persia, Greece, and Rome. Instead of the parts of the image's body, weren't the kingdoms represented by beasts?"

"Yes, that's right. A lion for Babylon. A bear for Medo-Persia. A leopard with four heads for Greece."

"What are the four heads for, Reuben?" interrupted Sabina.

"When Alexander the Great died, he had no son to leave his kingdom to, so it was divided among his four generals."

"My land!" exclaimed Sabina. "The prophecy is as accurate as *that!*"

"Yes, that's what sort of gets me, Sabina. You see, the last kingdom was a beast they called great and terrible. Here, let me read it. Is the Bible over there?"

Sabina brought him the Bible and sat down with a great basket of mending right near. She was touched to note that Aunt Zinnia, who was clearing the supper table, was listening carefully.

"This is in verse twenty-three of the seventh chapter of Daniel," Reuben answered. Then he turned his chair a little so that he could catch the light all the better.

"'Thus he said, The fourth beast shall be the fourth kingdom upon earth, which shall be diverse from all kingdoms, and shall devour the whole earth, and shall tread it down, and break it in pieces. And the ten horns out of this kingdom are ten kings that shall arise: and another shall rise after them; and he shall be diverse from the first, and he shall subdue three kings. And he shall speak great words against the most High, and shall wear out the saints of the most High, and think to change times and laws: and they shall be given into his hand until a time and times and the dividing of time.'"

"What does that mean, Reuben?"

"Well, it means that that smaller horn out of Rome was going to do a lot of things. One of them, it was going to wear out the saints—give the people of God a bad time, I take it. Then that same power that grew out of Rome was going to make an attempt to change times and laws."

"You mean that the law of God was tampered with, Reuben?"

"We will have to face it, Sabina; it surely was. Have you ever wondered why we do not keep the old Sabbath—the Jewish one—that falls on the seventh day of the week and is called Saturday?"

"Why, they say that it passed away, that we keep the first day to commemorate Jesus' resurrection."

"But Jesus was a commandment-keeper, the way I see it, and a Sabbathkeeper. Listen to what I read from a book written by Eusebius, who was a friend of the Roman Emperor Constantine: 'All things whatsoever that was duty to do on the Sabbath, these we have transferred to the Lord's day.' The way it seems to me, neither Constantine nor anyone else has any right to tamper with God's law. Look here at this page. Here is how the law was as God gave it to us. Here is how it was changed."

"Why, they have left out the second commandment. I wonder why?"

"That was a commandment that forbade the bowing down to images."

"Oh, I see. And look. The fourth is really shortened. It says, 'Remember to keep holy the Sabbath day.' But where do they make ten, if they leave out one, Reuben?"

"They divided the tenth, and that makes two about covetousness. We can't get around it, Sabina. The day most people keep is not the right day."

"I don't see what we can do about that," Sabina answered. "Though I am stubborn enough to

8   113

wish I could. But what does it mean there where it says they will wear out the saints, or something?"

Reuben looked at his wife appreciatively. Still beautiful. But with a plump matronliness that added to her charm. Smart as a whip, too. He felt sorry for some men who could not talk things over with their wives. Silly empty heads who thought of nothing but clothes, and the price of butter and mutton and eggs.

"Well, this book I got in New York——" Reuben got up and opened a volume at a place he had marked—"it's by Lecky. It says the fact that 'the Church of Rome has shed more innocent blood than any other institution that has ever existed among mankind will be questioned by no Protestant who has a complete knowledge of history. The memorials, indeed of many of her persecutions are now so scanty that it is impossible to form a complete conception of the multitude of her victims, and it is quite certain that no powers of imagination can adequately realize their sufferings. These atrocities were not perpetrated in brief paroxysms of a reign of terror, or by the hands of obscure sectaries, but

114

were inflicted by a triumphant church, with every circumstance of solemnity and deliberation.' "

"How terrible!" Sabina answered. "But I have heard of that before. We had an old book by Fox about things like that. When daddy read it aloud, I would run to the bedroom and bury my head in the feather bed. He told me once that I reminded him of an ostrich. Just because I would not hear truth did not change it any."

"I have read that book myself. And the same power that did that persecuting was the power that changed the Sabbath of the Lord into Sunday. At least that is what Uriah Smith brings out in his book."

"Reuben, I am almost sorry that we ever saw that book!" declared Sabina. "It gets us all stirred up, and I don't know a thing we can do about it."

"Humph!" snorted Aunt Zinnia from the depths of the buttery. "Y'all plannin' on stickin' yo' haid inter a fedder bed agin, Mis Sabina?" With that the old colored woman, carrying a great load of washing which she wanted to get started at early, opened the back door and left.

Reuben laughed. Then he stood up and looked down at his wife's flushed face. Then he sobered up and looked off across the room for a moment. His face seemed unutterably sad.

"I am afraid the whole thing is all too true," he told Sabina. "I decided not to say a word about this till I had run down every clue I could find. I spent every spare minute on the train and in the hotel searching the Bible for proof that the day was divinely changed. And it is not there. If it had been, I'd have found it. But I found plenty of proof that the apostles kept the Sabbath clear down to the end of the Bible. And if it is not in the Bible that the day is changed, it has to be man-made—and it is."

"Reuben, don't we keep the day—as I've heard all my life—because Christ arose from the dead on that day?"

"No, we don't," Reuben answered quietly. "That's only a lame excuse for continuing to keep a day that Rome instituted. I know, Sabina. I looked this up carefully."

"But the resurrection, darling!" his wife cried, visibly troubled at this seeming menace that ap-

116

peared to threaten the very tenor of their lives. "Why can't it be proper and beautiful to have a memorial to the resurrection?"

"We *do*," Reuben answered her. "The ceremony of baptism, preceded by repentance. When we go down into the water and are baptized with the Bible baptism—not sprinkling or pouring—we have a memorial to His death, burial, and resurrection. Repentance and conversion is the death to sin. Baptism is the burial and the resurrection into a new life."

"But what, pray tell, is the old Jewish Sabbath a memorial of, dear?" Sabina asked, marveling inwardly at the way her husband had gone into all these hard subjects.

"That," Reuben said, "I got out of the book *Thoughts on Daniel*. The seventh-day Sabbath is the memorial of the creation of the world. That is where the seven-day week comes from. When God began His work, there was no Sabbath; but there was one when He finished His work, and He rested on it."

They had gotten so interested that they had not noted the passage of time. They had to go to bed, for the hands of the clock stood almost at the hour of midnight. But both of them were troubled when they sought their rest. For they were earnest and good, both of them, and they had never yet in their married life turned their faces from any duty that they thought was right and good. Reuben had laughed at Sabina's statement that she wished they had never seen the book, but he had the same feeling several times but had dismissed it as an unworthy thought. For it was surely bringing up problems in their lives they had not dreamed of having to meet. Their little family, the store, Pop Conners, the whole community. It was not a decision that would touch their lives and their lives alone.

Nothing much was said about it for a few days, though it was on the minds of both. The studies were in the Book of Revelation now, and it seemed to Sabina as she sat and listened to Reuben read that the truth of the Sabbath was on every page. And so it seemed to Reuben. Even Mr. Bankhead noted it and spoke about it to Reuben.

"What do you and Sabiny think of what this feller says about keepin' Sunday, Reuben?" the old man asked one day as he called at the Pelman home.

"Well, it says here that it is the 'mark of the beast,' doesn't it?" Reuben answered, evading the direct question. But Mr. Bankhead was not to be side-stepped.

"Yes, I know," he said in his quavery old voice. "I know what it says, and it is troubling me. I say, What are you and Sabiny goin' to do about it?"

Sabina directed a question to her husband: "Reuben, if this *is* true, what can we do? Pa Conners will never consent to having his store closed on Saturday. You know we sell more on Saturday than we sell on all the other days of the week put together. Pa is *good*, but you know how dogmatic he is about Sunday."

Old Bankhead laughed a high cackling laugh. "Ye hadn't ort to have all yer holdin's in pa's hands, Reub," he said. "Everyone knows they're yours, well, really more'n they are pa's. A feller like you hadn't ort to be at the beck and call of anyone else as far as his follerin' what he thinks is right."

Reuben looked at the old man and realized all too clearly that all that he said was true. Why should he, who had worked like a slave, be afraid to do

119

anything he considered to be the right thing to do? Then he answered Mr. Bankhead and Sabina.

"I haven't decided yet. But I will say, it has me worried. If we are doing nothing but following pop-ery in keeping Sunday, I do not want any of it."

"I don't think it's right to work seven days a week, Reuben," offered Mr. Bankhead, "but, hon-estly, I can't git it through my head what difference it makes."

Reuben got up and walked back and forth a few minutes before he answered. Then he stood in front of the old man.

"Sir," he said, "you told me the other day that your birthday is on Christmas Day. You said you got cheated, for folks gave you just one present and let it do for both. If you don't like your birthday on Christmas, why don't you change it? A fellow *has* to have a birthday, and I don't see why you don't have it in June or July—as far from Christmas as you can get it. That would solve all your problems."

"Aw, go on, Reub. 'Twouldn't either. Fust place, 'twouldn't *be* my birthday, and if a feller is goin' t' have a birthday, it better be on the right day."

"Exactly," Reuben answered. "The Sabbath is the birthday of creation, and if we celebrate it on the first day, it can't be true, for that was the day God started, not the day He ended it."

"Reuben," Sabina said, "if everyone had kept the Sabbath, there would hardly be any legs for infidels to stand on. Every week they would be reminded of the creation week."

"That's right, and I, for one, do not see how *any* church, no matter how powerful, has the right to change the direct commands of God. And they can't really change it any more than you can change your birthday. It is as plain as that."

"Way I see it," Mr. Bankhead remarked as he arose to leave, "if it's all right and good fer man to change and twist around the things that were writ there in the Scripter, there ain't no tellin' where they might twist it around to make it legal and right to kill and steal. Can't trust a body as does things like that. Fer my money, I say, let the Word o' God alone."

They Leave the Old Home

SABINA AND REUBEN studied the matter for several days before Reuben decided to lay the matter before Pa Conners. They knew that pa was pretty dogmatic, but they were not prepared for the violent reaction from the usually mild and kind old man. He fairly grew livid with rage. He arose trembling and vehemently shook an old finger in Reuben's face.

"Ye cain't do that there to me," he shrilled. "I won't let ye work in my stores or have a thing if ye go off on sich a foolish religion as that. Oh, I been hearin' things, I have, but I didn't give 'em any mind, fer I thought ye had more sense than what Mr. Bankhead has been tellin' all over the country-

122

"You can't do this to me and ma!" he shouted.

side. Me and ma told him you'd have more sense than to keep Sat'day fer Sunday."

Reuben noted with great pity the trembling blue-veined old hands. His heart went out to pa, for he had received many bounties and much love at his and ma's hands, and he knew it very well. But this matter of being tied by the bands of dogmatism was not pleasing to Reuben's honest soul, either. But he saw that pa was in no mind for reason. So he merely stood there and said not a thing.

"I'll cut you off without a cent!" he shouted. Reuben thought sickly that he could do just that if he wanted to, for he had trusted the old man implicitly, even though a little bell of fear had sounded more than once in his practical heart.

While he stood there, the old man leaped out of his chair, and paced to and fro, excitedly. "You can't do this to me and ma!" he shouted, punctuating his words by banging excitedly on the counter. "You get this fool Sat'day notion out o' yer head, 'r git out!"

Ma Conners had come in and was alarmed first. Now she was weeping aloud, her white face buried in her snowy apron.

"Oh, Pa, don't talk that way to Reuben. Don't ye remember how he has been so good to us? Don't ye remem——"

"I been a friend t' him, too," he thundered, his sparse beard waggling in anger. "He wouldn't 'a' had a thing—not a thing—if he hadn't built it up on my cap'tal, my stock, and my prop'ty. I took him in—rags, skin, bones, and prison sores, and made him what he is."

"Oh, Pa," ma sobbed, "Reuben's toiled and worked early and late never countin' hours on us, and made our interest first. He——"

"Silence!" pa screamed at her. "You get back to the kitchen where ye belong. Me and Reuben, we'll settle this."

"Look, Pa." Reuben folded his arms and stood up. He was tall and earnest. Ma from the doorway, through scalding tears, thought how fair and pretty he was. "Listen to me for a minute." Reuben was saddened immeasurably at the state the poor old man had worked himself into. His pity even took precedence over the alarm he felt at losing all he had worked for for years. "I took the things I read from

125

the Bible as a revelation from God," he said as gently as he could. "Sabina and I have thought over this for a long time, and we feel like it is truth. And you know, Pa, I always was fair and honest with you; I want to be fair and honest with God."

"He has, too," wept ma; "he has. He has done fer us like a son, not like a duty. Let him do his duty to God, Pa. Don't ye make it hard fer him."

"Duty? Fiddlesticks!" snapped pa angrily. "Ain't you thought of your duty to me? Me, who made ye all ye are?"

Reuben, looking into pa's angry face realized the futility of an argument. He'd like to have pointed out the long, long hours of the years spent on the road, building up the shattered business. Of the hunger, the cold, and the privation he had cheerfully endured to start over again and make a place that pa had repeatedly told him would be his someday.

Now it seemed it would not be his. Not unless he was willing to sell his conscience for what pa had honestly promised. All of a sudden he remembered the first chapter of Daniel. Daniel decided to do the right thing even though it meant a threat to his very life. This posed no threat to his life, only a change of birthrights; the portion he had thought to be his would not be his. He stood there, heartsick at the thought.

Pa looked up and saw in Reuben's strong face his answer.

"All right, Reuben. Take the money in the bank, and the team, and get out. I will not trust even the store where you are to a fanatic like you. My nephew will be the manager of the store where you are from now on." Then pa turned and walked out, leaving Reuben standing, stunned, looking after him. Alger! And pa would add insult to injury by putting Alger into the store he had labored so hard to build up. It was utterly unbelievable. Reuben knew that Alger always blamed him because pa had not let him work for him any more. Pa knew Alger was a thief and lazy and absolutely irresponsible. Everyone in town knew that. Reuben knew he could fight pa through the courts and perhaps get an accounting, but he was so heartsick, he did not want it that way. He would rather by far start from scratch, even though the whole thing was grossly unjust.

Reuben turned and went out, hitched the horse, and started for home, as sad and bewildered as he was years before when he first came to this part of the country.

Pa had never meant a word he said about Alger, ma's sister's worthless son. He well knew, without anyone telling him, the young man was a general good-for-nothing. He would never be able to abide him any more than Reuben could. But he had foolishly thought to scare Reuben into giving up what he honestly thought was a pack of foolishness. Keeping Saturday for Sunday! Who ever heard of such a thing? But that night, he thought to let Reuben sweat. Let him think he meant all he said. Let him think it. He told ma what he had in mind, but she only wept louder.

"He won't never come back, Pa," she wailed. "He won't give up, if he think's he's right, and I dunno but what he might be. You 'n me we ain't never studied in the Bible er found out anythin' fer ourselves."

"Jew Sabbath!" Pa spat, as if there had been a toad in his mouth.

128

"Jes' the same, Pa, don't ye fergit that Jesus was a Jew, and so was them other fellers as wrote the Bible. You never give Reuben a chanct to explain hisself. It fair wrenched my soul seein' him there sad-like fer all the world like our Charlie."

"Ma, you see; he'll be back at the crack o' dawn in the mornin'. And I'm goin' t' the lawyer in the mornin' and make over all I got t' Reuben. I guess I hadn't ort t' talked s' mean 'n hateful to him."

When pa had eaten supper and the enormity of what he had done began to dawn upon him, he knew that he had been most unjust and cruel. If there had been telephones, he'd have had Reuben on the phone right away, but Alexander Graham Bell's wonderful invention was not in general use yet. Many people had never seen it, though Reuben had seen a few when on his trips to New York and Washington.

Pa knew that if it had not been for Reuben and his enormous energy, schemes, and tireless labor, he would never have been able to have gone beyond the ramshackle shop Reuben had first helped him to build up. All that he had said was most unjust and

9 129

cruel. He could hardly sleep that night. He trembled and talked to ma most of the night. When it began to lighten up, and ma knew it was almost morning, she got up and started to stir up the fireplace so she could brew him a good cup of hot tea. She was not gone more than twenty or twenty-five minutes. When she returned, she could not believe her own eyes. Pa Conners was dead!

In the days that followed ma was so beside herself that the neighbors shook their heads sadly. Some said that the sod would not be grown on pa's grave before she would be lying beside him. And how true this statement proved to be, for in just a few weeks good and patient ma was laid to rest beside the still fresh mound of pa's resting place.

Alger Collinsmith got everything. All that Reuben had worked so hard to achieve was in the hands of a worthless wastrel. One of the first things he did was to set up a bar in one end of pa's original store. What temperate old pa would have said if he had known would not be hard to guess.

Reuben and Sabina had their house and the money they had saved. That was all. Alger bought the house from them and paid cash for it. And so the once-thriving couple pulled up stakes and moved away from the house they had loved so much. They were glad to get away from the place where such a glaring injustice was done to them.

"To think," he told Sabina, when they were getting settled in their new home, "to think of such a thing happening to me—me. Why, I always thought that I knew all the pitfalls and mistakes enough to avoid them all. Now look at us." And he laughed a little ruefully.

"We have our health, and we have such good, bright children," Sabina said. "We also have a will to start again. It may be God has some other path laid out for our feet."

"One of the most wonderful things we have is our conscience—our right to do right as we see it to do right."

"Yes, that's so," Sabina answered.

Reuben had chosen the place where they now lived almost on the spur of the moment. He had seen it for sale once when he had been on a buying trip. He had considered it even then as a possible third store for pa, but the old man was timorous about spreading his wings too far. He did not have the youth or the courage that Reuben had, and now Reuben was glad they had not taken the step.

The place they bought with the money they had saved was a fine farm—almost four hundred acres— and it lay right on the edge of a small town. The house had stood empty for a long time and was not in such good repair, but basically it was good and solid. Off in one corner of the great lawn, a doctor had built a sizable building for offices and had a room or two built on the back, presumably for his helper to live in. Here was where Reuben determined to make a store. By tearing out some partitions, he felt it was almost ideal. He drew plans, and they pored over them for several hours that night in the lamplight.

"With the farm, we will have a living for the boys when they grow up and set out for themselves," Reuben told Sabina excitedly. "We just have to look ahead, Sabina."

Sabina agreed. Yes, with growing children, one just has to look ahead. He just has to see to it that

132

he builds without a possible chance of failure. He has to be absolutely sure he is right. Or does he? Or could he?

Reuben had gone into their bedroom and was laboriously screwing on the massive top to the ornate headboard of their bed. The sweat poured down his face as the lamplight flickered in the old, old room. Their shadows were long and ghostly, and Sabina thought how boylike Reuben looked, how pathetic, stripped of all that he had owned in almost a day. And a great anger surged over her. What right had fate—or Pa Conners, or war, or famine, or failure of any kind—to steal sixteen years right out of a man's life? Ma had protested that pa had said the quarrel between Reuben and pa had meant nothing, that pa wanted Reuben to have everything, but they had not listened to her. There had been no will. If pa had wanted Reuben to have had anything, he would have made it out to him, so the law said. Now he was cheated because he had sought to do the will of God. It was not right. It was the fourth of a whole lifetime. Where was God that He would let this happen to Reuben? Reuben who had tried so hard and been so good. Wasn't Reuben ever to have his portion?

In spite of all the feeling that must have been in his heart, Reuben hid it from his family and kept a serene, even happy appearance before his family. He and Reuben Junior and Joseph got lumber and built shelves and counters in the new store room. Young Reuben was the image of his father, even to the steady look in his eyes and the sideways grin; but Joseph, only a year and a half younger, was almost a head taller than his brother. His hair was black, and his eyes were a deep wine brown. While the sawing and hammering were going on in the storeroom, eleven-year-old Benjamin and nine-year-old Ephraim were busy cleaning out the big log barn for the livestock that Reuben would soon be trading for—that is, as soon as the store got going.

The very week that they were getting settled, a letter came from Sabina's mother, who had not been too understanding of the whole thing. She could not see a lick of sense in all that commotion over a silly thing like which day of the week is the right day to rest. As if a silly thing like that made any difference to God. Sabina tried to explain, but to no avail. The letter was uninteresting to Reuben to say the least. Part of it read as follows:

"Well, Alger has sure been running things in a sorry state here at the store, and I hear that things are in one grand mixup in the other store too. He's not tending to any business, but the bar, and he is his own best customer there. He told me the other day, he'd be glad to hire you, Reuben, to come and manage both stores for him. He said to come any time. I hope you do swallow your pride and come, for I miss the children so much. Rose and Lily will forget all about us."

Reuben read this the day he got his store all ready to open. He had secured a fine stock, and things looked pretty nice. But the letter touched a tender spot in his heart. He almost felt like weeping to think that all that he and poor old pa had worked for so hard was going so fast. Well, it did not take long. He had not felt so terrible since he stood long ago before the rubble that had once been his home. Now, he stood before another ruin. Another portion of his life was in shambles. It was a part that he had trusted to be his portion—Reuben's portion. Now that, too, had crumbled away. Was he to have no portion?

135

He looked around at the new store, clean with new lumber and paint. Barrels of coffee, sugar—soft and the color of old ivory—stood by more coffee bags of green coffee, ready for the thrifty housewife who roasted and ground her own. There were kits of mackerel and a few kegs of bluefish, a barrel of vinegar and a barrel of coal oil. There were candles for the women who did not save "taller" to make their own. Saleratus, bolts of cloth, needles, pins, a slab of salt cod on the counter, shoes, salt, tea, young hyson, and gunpowder—all these were on sale.

One end of the store held hardware and not a few dishes, iron pots, skillets, dippers, and buckets. A few kegs of nails of various sizes stood next to the brand-new counter. Sabina told Reuben that she would not be a bit surprised if they would not have a post office there before the year was out.

Of course Reuben would have nothing to do with Alger's offer. He could never work with Alger, as given as he was to unjust dealings, and as often as he got drunk. Sabina's mother ought to know that. No one could work with Alger and hope to get any kind of square deal. And, of course, he would be expected

136

to work in the bar as well as the store. The reason for the rift with pa still existed, and Alger kept the stores open seven days a week.

Reuben and Sabina thought they had a wonderful store, and so did the boys. If they could have walked into the marvels of chromium and tile and gleaming tons of merchandise of the modern supermarket, they would have been lost for words. In place of the cold-storage counters of frozen foods of all types, Reuben's only concession was the great slab of salted codfish, stiff and glistening. There were no bright cans of fruits or vegetables, for a woman who did not get a lot of apples and "punkin" and peaches dried during the summer was hardly worthy to be called a housewife. These dried foods were to be used for pie fillings after the fruits which had been stored in the cellar had become too mellow and even rotten to be any longer so used.

Along the top of the glass case where he had combs, pins, scissors, needles, and notions was a row of candy jars, tall and new. Here were stored items of great interest to the children—notably Rose and Lily. There were several kinds of stick candy—

horehound, peppermint, wintergreen—and one canister was full of cinnamon drops that the children called "red-hots." Another had white peppermint drops in it that the children called "grampa candy" because it was the only candy favored by Sabina's kind old father. They were as round as a nickel, and many times thicker, and had four X's printed on their fat chalk-white sides.

Keen Competition

REUBEN AND SABINA talked it over, and after much indecision and discussion, pro and con, they decided to keep their store open on Saturday at the first, and let the people get acquainted with them before they "sprung" some queer and strange religious ideas on them. They were both very earnest about this, and thought most honestly that they were doing what was right and good.

But here they made their first mistake. They did not realize the life-and-death matter about truth. They did not realize that opening their store on Saturday just to get acquainted and then later closing it on that day would be like cutting a dog's tail off a little at a time so it would not hurt so much. Even Reuben, their thoughtful fourteen-year-old son, looked sober over their decision.

"Don't seem quite logical to me," he offered. "You have a big break-up with pa and leave in a hurry—and everyone back home knows good and well why—then you come here, and don't take the very stand you stood out for. Looks like if you wanted to do it at pa's store, you ought to be able to trust God enough to try it in your own."

Reuben hardly knew how to answer that logic, which he knew in his heart of hearts was sound and right. He tried to explain to the clear-eyed boy that he fully aimed to take his stand—at the right time. But he rather felt that he better get things to going first. Sabina was silent, for she shared the views of their oldest son. But her arguments seemed weak and unworkable before Reuben's.

"You better let me work it out, Sabina," he had said kindly yet firmly. "I mustn't make a mistake this time. I want to build so there will not be a chance of failure; I don't want to make the mistakes that some people make. I want to build solidly; we have these children to think about." Reuben stopped shortly

140

and looked at Sabina. She was looking at him pecu-
liarly. He realized that he was saying the very things
he had reiterated again and again during their life
together. And no one had made much more of a failure in good solid judgment than he had. But he felt
so sure that he was right that he turned away and
went into the store.

Reuben spoke truly so far as one thing was concerned. It was a good location. And it was not long
until the place was a buzzing beehive of activity.
Sheep bleated in hastily made pens out by the log
barn. Calves bawled, and chickens and turkeys fat-
tened and sang themselves into a frenzy laying eggs.
Reuben, beside himself with joy at the success of
his venture, was on the road almost continually. Sabina and a neighbor woman and man kept store. The
boys chored around after school; Aunt Zinnia kept
the girls in tow and the housework done. But she
shook her wise old head many times during those
first few months.

Before the year was out, they felt well enough
established to step out and keep the Sabbath as they
firmly believed it to be. Up to this time, they had not

seen another Sabbathkeeper, so they felt that they were doing a brave and pioneer thing. Since it was the only store for miles around, Reuben felt reasonably safe. But he had not counted on the caliber of the enemy. Reuben had given him plenty of time to marshal his forces.

The whole thing transpired in a place so bigoted and so narrow-minded that a few years later several Sabbathkeepers were jailed for breaking the so-called Lord's day. But Reuben could not foretell the future; he felt he had built solidly. He figured to get his reputation established first, make a place for himself in the hearts of the people, and then they would overlook any peculiarities that he might display later on. He could not have acted with poorer judgment. He had not yet learned the lessons that God must teach every child who is learning to serve him. He had not yet learned to allow God first place in his life. He was always determined to wait for the most auspicious moment and choose just when and how he would obey. He endeavored to soften the blows and to ward off future disaster. But one thing he overlooked: Satan was also hard at work.

Alger Collinsmith, angered beyond measure because Reuben had refused to come back and do the "dirty work" and keep the stores prospering while he played the "big boss," was waiting patiently, yea, even a little impatiently, for the right moment. He knew that Reuben had not immediately put into practice what he professed to believe, and he craftily divined the reason. He was reasonably sure that in the course of time he would make a try at it. So he set to work.

There was a half-ruined store building in the same town where Reuben had his store, though it had stood empty since someone tried to set up a drugstore there and failed. The very week that Reuben started keeping the Sabbath, Alger rented this place, hastily moved a stock of goods over from Creek Center, and started up a rival store.

Then began a most insidious whispering campaign. In a pious whine, and with sundry dark and devious hints, and without actually openly accusing, the gossips had it that Reuben had cruelly pulled away and left poor old Pa Conners while he was virtually on his deathbed. Yes, sir. Actually was hard and unpitying enough to leave him the very day before he died. That was a pity, for everyone at Conners could tell how pa and ma had all but taken Reuben and treated him like a son. The poor old man had drained his lifeblood for Reuben and only found he was nursing a viper at his bosom.

People, ever ready to believe the worst, and surprised and confused at the closing of the store on Saturday, and angered at its being open on Sunday, decided to boycott Reuben's store, until he could learn some sense. Alger was behind the whole thing, and so was the devil.

The queer and strange thing was that neither Reuben nor Sabina realized that there was a church which believed as they did about the seventh-day Sabbath. They felt themselves to be pioneers in doing the thing they were doing. In a sense they were, for at that time there were no Sabbathkeepers in that part of the state. But Reuben, writing a letter to Battle Creek to inquire whether they had any other books such as the one that changed his whole life, learned differently. In the course of a few weeks he had added to his library considerably. Four volumes by Mrs. E. G. White got them so curious that they had to buy a book called *Life Sketches*. They learned then of the large number of people who were keeping the Bible Sabbath and looking for the Lord to come.

They purchased another wonderful thing, too. A four-volume set of books of stories, interesting and instructive, called *Sabbath Readings for the Home Circle,* arrived, much to even sober, serious young Reuben's delight. Reuben got the *History of the Sabbath,* by J. N. Andrews, a good man, they told him in a letter from Battle Creek, who had gone to Switzerland as a missionary a few years before.

But the little family, in spite of the delights of some things, were plunged into great perplexity on the other hand. With Alger's store, which was not nearly so clean, not so complete, nor so well managed, but where gossip, scurrilous and untrue, was doled out with the staples, Reuben's trade dropped to a dribble. Also, Alger started up a bar, and although he had it in the back room, it certainly attracted the element which Reuben had never catered to. He also dealt in tobacco, which Reuben had decided not to sell. Then Reuben realized fully what was happening. But it was too late to do a thing. If he had had the money to move far away, so far that even Alger would not know where he went, he might make it. But he did not have the money.

About this time some visitors arrived—J. O. Corliss and S. H. Lane. Reuben found to his joy that they were ministers and believers in the coming of the Lord. Sabina and Aunt Zinnia made them comfortable in a great guest room they had had no occasion to use until then. They were to stay over the Sabbath. Aunt Zinnia was all smiles. And she went to the smokehouse to select the finest ham that was hanging there so that there would be nothing left undone to make their breakfast the delight of their hungry souls. The slab of home-cured bacon, with the widest streak of lean, was carried proudly in and set in readiness on the shelf of the pantry. Coffee was roasted and ground in the little mill that Aunt Zinnia held on her lap. She turned it vigorously, emptying the little drawer as fast as it got full.

But when the week end was over, Sabina and Reuben still marveled over the new things they had learned. They had not known there were whole

146

chapters in the Old Testament telling the children of Israel just what meats were good for them to eat, and naming others as unclean and so unfit for food that man was told not to even touch them. These men told them that a number of people were considering letting all meats alone. Then they got some brown books out of their book satchels and showed them some quotations written by Mrs. White. One was from a letter that was written to the medical institution that was then operated in Battle Creek. It said, "A positive injury is done to the system by continuous meat eating. There is no excuse for it but a depraved, perverted appetite. You may ask, would you do away entirely with meat eating? I answer, it will eventually come to this, but we are not prepared for this step just now. Meat eating will eventually be done away."

Reuben was interested in that, and Sabina had him tell the brethren about his experience in the war when he had nothing to eat except vegetables. Then they told of people who came to the Battle Creek Sanitarium from all over the world and went away in wonderful health. They told of the great

147

"You ol' dirty hawgs, I ain't gonna mek cannibals outa you,"
and she raked the ham away from them.

building, even then in process of construction, that would be the largest of its kind in the world.

Aunt Zinnia went and threw the ham to the hogs. Then, on a second thought, she got a hoe and raked it out and buried it, saying as she did so, "I tell you, you ol' dirty hawgs, I ain't gonna mek cannibals outa you even though you are scavengahs of de 'arth. You all can't eat you' brothahs heah, right whah Zinnia ken see you."

Reuben, who was forking out the stable nearby, was so amused that he went and told Sabina all that she said. The little family began then to eliminate from their diet all the foods that the Lord told the children of Israel were unfit for food.

Reuben, of course, brought up the argument that he wondered whether the Lord had not meant that those things were ceremonies for the Jews alone, but both Pastor Corliss and Pastor Lane laughed at that idea.

"Do you think the pig is any cleaner today than he was back there?" asked one of them. Then Reuben remembered a few days before when young Reuben had killed a young rattlesnake in the woods

lot. He had come bringing it home on a forked stick.
After he had showed it around, one of the shoats,
who had wriggled under the fence of the sty, came
by and made short work of the serpent, much to the
lad's disgust.

Then, with all the other things they had decided
to do, before the two good men went on their way,
Reuben and Sabina decided to give up unclean and
unwholesome foods. They did not tell the visitors of
the crisis coming into their lives, for Reuben coun-
seled Sabina against it. "Things may turn out better than we think, and then we would feel foolish.
Anyway, it is a thing we will have to battle out for
ourselves."

In spite of all that they could do, their worst fears
were soon realized. Customers seldom came into the
store. Local religious groups, antagonized, urged the
boycotting of the store and the patronizing of Alger
Collinsmith's store until such a time as "Mr. Pelman
comes to his senses." After several weeks of no trade
at all, Reuben wept great shaking sobs, until even
the little girls and Aunt Zinnia were wailing aloud.
Sabina had never seen him so, and she too was

Sabina had never seen Reuben so shaken.

shaken. She walked around the table and put her arms around her husband.

"Don't, Reuben, dear," she said, sobs catching at her throat too. "See, you have the little girls and Aunt Zinnia all upset. God has got a lesson in this for us, you see. Let's just pray a little more and find out what His will is for us."

"God has forgotten us, Sabina," Reuben said brokenly. Joseph, the second son, shrewd for his years, came around and put his hand on his mother's arm. He had just come in from the barn. His face was dirty, so his tears had made a few irregular traces down his young face.

Reuben Junior came in then, too, from the barn, carrying two big buckets of foamy milk. He was followed by Benjamin, who had helped milk.

"The way I see it," Joseph said, his young voice breaking with his emotion, "seems like we are the ones who have done the forgetting. You folks broke loose from pa about the Sabbath, then came here and broke it for a long time, just like you could not trust God to make a way for you to do it—I mean—well——"

152

"Yes." Young Reuben had set the buckets down, and sensing the trend of the conversation, gave his contribution on the subject under discussion. "Benjamin and I both thought you ought to have started right away, didn't we, Benjie? We talked about it that very first week. I kinda think we've given the devil a little time to get up his army, and we're in for more trouble than if we had started right in the first place." Aunt Zinnia's loud sigh, half a hiccup, from the kitchen was her voice of agreement with what had been said.

Reuben had poured out a panful of warm water and was lathering his face and arms. Ephraim came in then and stood in line for his ablution. Reuben said, "If we'd started just as soon as we got here, people would not have thought half so much about it. They'd be used to it by now, and Alger would never have had his chance."

Sabina had cleared the table to set it for the supper. She looked up proudly at her boys. They were so clean, so noble, and so good, so ready to help shoulder the problems of a family, to search out the solution.

"The boys are right, Reuben," she said simply. From the doorway Aunt Zinnia looked the picture of dolefulness and was dishing up the mush with many sighs. Rose and Lily were the only members of the family unaffected by the crisis. They already had their mush bowls and were whispering and giggling to each other. They were both absorbed with the sorghum jug and the maple sugar bowl and were discussing which one tasted the best on corn meal mush, with cream and butter added.

When the whole family had gathered around the table at last, they were so downhearted and glum looking that the two little girls looked around the table and from face to face in great astonishment. But in a moment with the complete trust of childhood, they were engrossed in the solid comfort of the good food.

"I'll tell you something." It was Ephraim who spoke up out of the silence. He had gotten enough of the conversation to hear his own bigger brothers' contributions, and he had determined to add his bit to it. "I think we ought to pray at the table, too, like Mr. Bankhead does. He told me wunst, 'at even the chickens lift up their heads towards heaven when they take a drink of water. They do, too. I watched 'em. He said that heathens don't ever thank God for what they eat, and he ain't gonna be like a heathen."

"I know," Benjamin contributed. "I heard Jim Wertz' father call it returnin' thanks t' God. They always do at their house, and teacher at the school prays before we open our lunch buckets."

"I think that's a good idea. Don't you, Daddy?" Sabina asked. "Some people call it 'saying grace,' and I have thought we ought to do it. But my folks never did, and I didn't exactly know how to begin."

Reuben looked up at this, the light of appreciation in his tired eyes. "I think it is a good idea," he said. "You remember those ministers prayed. I sort of expected them to—but——"

"Well, if we don't know how, we might as well begin," Sabina said with forced cheerfulness. "Now Rose, you and Lily must not start eating after this till we have asked God to bless our food."

It was a lame, awkward beginning, but they all felt better, and the cloud of gloom seemed to lift.

But things seemed to go from bad to worse. Yet, let it be said to Reuben's credit, that he never once dreamed of going back on the truth as he found it in the book. Finally both he and Sabina realized they were "licked." They could not continue. They had to have some resources, even though none of them had gone hungry. They both concluded that God evidently did not want them to be in that place or doing that particular thing. They had more hard lessons to learn before they realized the judgments of the Lord are true and righteous altogether.

They had learned the real meaning of prayer by this time. They prayed with deep agony of soul and out of their great need. One day the answer came, and it was so plain that even the boys and Aunt Zinnia concurred that it must have been an answer from the Lord.

One day an insultingly low offer came from Alger, for all that Reuben owned. On the very same day a well-to-do lawyer came and gave cash for the farm, stock, and all that Reuben possessed. They had a loss, yes, a considerable one, counting everything, but not as much as they had been afraid of. Then

Reuben went to see a farm that was offered for sale some miles away. He came back all aglow and enthusiastic. It was a large farm but almost entirely undeveloped. There was a wonderful river running through it, but very little of it was cleared. There was a big barn and a large hewed-log house. A great step-down from the roomy, gracious home they had fitted out with so much pleasure and anticipation a few short months before. But this was what Reuben was so glad about: In the nearest town was a small church of Sabbathkeepers. His voice almost broke with emotion when he told the assembled family, all of whom were packing madly. Aunt Zinnia had been weeping all day. One of her daughters-in-law had died back in Conners, and she had to go back and take charge of her son's family of eight little children, the youngest of which was only eight days old. So they had to take the move without her kindly help. She seemed almost like one of the family.

The last night they spent in the house they had bought with such high hopes was not particularly sad, for the children were all agog with the idea of moving. The boys had been told of a fine swimming

157

hole in the river just below the barn, and Reuben
told them that there were still bears to be seen in
that part of the country. As he got ready for bed that
last night, he laughed a little ruefully, but Sabina
noted that he was not so discouraged as he had been.
There was a different note to his voice, a note of hope
again. Sabina rejoiced to hear it.

"This is a far cry from the riches you and I determined to accumulate," he said.

"Yes," Sabina returned. "And we were the ones
who were not going to make a mistake. Well, Reuben, we have made as many and as bad ones as anyone ever did."

"Yes, and the worst one of all was to hold off doing the will of God."

"We were like that old king Paul tried to per-
suade—you know Pastor Corliss read to us about—
he wanted a more convenient time."

"I guess we have to keep learning," Reuben told
her boyishly. "I always tell myself, when I make a
mistake, 'Oh, I'll never make that mistake again.'
But I up and make another one just as bad—or worse,
maybe."

A Touchy Subject

THE NEXT DAY, with the two big farm wagons loaded full of household gear and other items they owned, with three good milk cows and a couple of coops of chickens and a few sheep, they started on the journey to the new home. The weather was so pleasant that the camping out and the cooking of the meals by the roadside was greatly enjoyed, especially by the children. On the evening of the third day, they drew into the front dooryard of the new home. They had barely time to fix up some beds on the floor and build up fires in the fireplace before night closed in. The two Reubens took care of the stock, even leading them down to drink by the cool waters of the river while Joseph, Benjamin, Ephraim, and Sabina did

what they could in the house. The two little girls
set up their family of dolls by the great fireplace, on
an old settee that the former tenants had not considered worth their taking. Ephraim, taking a lighted
candle up the stairs, its flame like a little fiery comet,
called down excitedly with the ring of an explorer
who had discovered a new land.

"Say, listen. We don't hafta sleep on the floor!"
he cried. "There's sever'l beds up here. I guess these
folks 'at owned this house was rich. Didn't even take
their stuff with 'em." The boys tugged the feather
beds up the stairs, and Sabina came up and soon had
the beds made. There were three bedrooms upstairs,
and in a little while the two little girls, having eaten
all the brown bread and milk they could hold, were
washed and put into the big billowy bed in the room
next to their parents.

The boys all felt that they were big enough to
wait and eat with the rest. Sabina had secured some
clabber milk that morning where they camped. She
had placed it in a linen bag and let it drain all day.
Now, emptied in a big bowl with rich, thick cream
added, they had smearcase—cottage cheese, their

160

grandchildren would call it. Sabina cooked a dozen eggs in the skillet over the fire and stirred up some fresh pone, which made them all think of good old Aunt Zinnia. With a dish of cream gravy as Sabina and Aunt Zinnia often made, they had a sumptuous banquet.

A table and chairs were already there, as well as a long food safe. The whole place was surprisingly clean. A long log pantry ran alongside the lean-to kitchen, where the huge fireplace was. The crane and the pot were there ready for use. There was a sizable fine brick oven at one side, with a place for a fire to be built underneath. Reuben would have to chisel into the big chimney for a hole for the stovepipe for the Farmer's Favorite, when he set it up. Even before they had brought in their things, it seemed like home. Reuben, eager as a boy, went over the whole place with Reuben Junior when they came in from the barn.

Then around the clean table, with grace said, they ate heartily—perhaps more heartily than if their plans had all gone to their liking and they had accumulated the wealth of their dreams.

11   161

The next few weeks were far more pleasant than they would have dreamed possible. The work was hard, and the days were filled with grueling toil. The boys went to school, but helped Reuben with his work as soon as they got home. Reuben racked his brain for ways to hasten the accumulation of a little money. Sabina made butter and cheese, and money from the sale of eggs they did not use went to buy the incidentals they could not raise on the little farm. Somehow, with the supplies they brought from their other place, they got through the winter. The biggest comfort they had was the church of eighteen members that met in the home of one of the members in Oak Valley, the nearest town. Once in a great while a minister came and talked to the members, but usually they got Reuben to read articles out of the *Review and Herald,* written by A. T. Jones, Mrs. White, or Uriah Smith. They got a club of *Youth's Instructor* Sabbath school papers, and the family read them from cover to cover every week. They sang from a songbook called the *Gospel Song Sheaf,* and Addie Springer played for the services on a fine parlor organ they had sent to Chicago to get.

But their clothes wore out, and the money from the sale of butter, eggs, and cheese was hardly sufficient to cover the things they actually needed. Many a night they did not light a lamp, but sat by the light of the open fire to save coal oil, for money was scarce. Reuben, who was accustomed to getting along better than most of the people around him, could hardly bear the role thrust upon him. It was not much comfort to him when he learned one day that Pa Conners's old store at Conners was sold by the sheriff and Alger was jailed as a member of a gang of highway robbers. He had been caught one night, with several others. It stirred Reuben, for he had known all along that Alger was rotten to the core. He had caught him with his own money box in his hands long before. His problem now still remained unsolved.

Hopefully he had put in the crops and worked early and late. He was out before sunrise and often did not come in until after dark. He grew thin, which caused Sabina to worry about him. He seemed determined to do well by his little family even if it killed him.

Always before when Reuben and the boys came in at night they were ravenously and healthily hungry. Sabina had good and tastily prepared food waiting for them. In other springs there had been dandelion greens, cooked and flavored with bacon or a piece of fat ham. But now the pork barrel that had figured so highly in their household needs was not even missed. The summer before, Sabina had "put up" literally bushels of blackberries, and the family knew no greater treat on a cold winter day than opening a can of blackberries to eat with Sabina's gingerbread, deliciously hot from her oven and flavored with sorghum from the jug that always sat in the corner of the kitchen near the fireplace.

Long before the Fourth of July, there were new peas and little new potatoes cooked together. If the wild strawberries were ripe, they had shortcake. Sabina made it in a long dripping pan, just like she made sour cream or buttermilk biscuits, only she made it a little shorter, and added a little molasses for sweetening. The berries all cleaned, drained, and sweetened, she mashed and set them aside until she split the fluffy fragrant cake, hot from the oven.

Slathering it with butter, until it ran in little rills
into the puffy center, she spooned the wild berries
onto the cake. The four boys, watching, hurriedly
ran to their places at the table so they need not wait
so long to eat. That, with cream so thick it had to be
spooned out of the squatty little pitcher, made a meal
fit for a king.

Sabina often made corndodgers—Benjamin's favorite bread—and all the family ate greedily when
they were on the table. She waited till she heard
them all at the barn, then she placed the rolls, the
size of goose eggs, into sizzling hot iron pans and
popped them into the oven. "So easy to make and so
good," she often thought as she put a pint of meal,
a tablespoonful of butter, a pinch of salt, and half
a pint of cold water straight from the spring into her
big bowl and beat it vigorously. "I have to keep it as
cold as I can," she thought. In the winter, she often
set her batter pan in a dishpan of snow. "That's their
secret," she told herself. "Their own steam raises
them, and it is cheaper than a yeast cake."

Money was still exceedingly hard to get. She got
only fifteen cents a pound for her delicious butter

and a nickel a gallon for buttermilk. Eggs were twelve cents a dozen.

That summer a tent was put up in the town of Oak Valley, and an evangelistic effort was held. Reuben and Sabina, tired as they were, drove in several nights a week. Sabina lent her organ, and young Reuben helped take care of the tent, which made him as proud as a peacock. Sabina played and Reuben helped to take up the offering. In later years both of them looked back on that summer as one of the happiest times of their lives. They worked hard, cruelly hard. Poor as they were, they always brought fresh things from the farm for the tent company as did many other friends.

Late in the summer a baptism was held in the river on Reuben and Sabina's farm. The boys had cleared the place and raked the approach until it looked like a park. A little church was established of twenty-six members. Reuben was made elder of the new company, and he negotiated with a firm who held an old church that had not been used for some years and succeeded in buying it at a bargain. It was of brick, and about a quarter of a mile from town. Bats were in the tower, and several of the windows were broken. But a little money and a lot of elbow grease can do wonders, so it was not long until the little company at Oak Valley had as neat a church as there was in the country.

A new problem now came up, a problem they had not heard much of before. It worried Reuben, especially since he had been made the elder of the new church. That was what the ministers in the tent had called the tithing system—giving a tenth of one's income to the Lord.

"I don't see how we can do that, Sabina," Reuben declared one day. "Why, we can just barely make it as it is. Now, take today—I took in ten pounds of butter."

"That's a dollar and a half," Joseph figured, looking up from the table where he was doing arithmetic. Reuben threw him an amused glance.

"Two gallons of buttermilk, a gallon of sweet milk."

"Plus twenty, that makes a dollar seventy." The boy's slate pencil scratched pleasantly while he figured carefully.

167

"And six dozen eggs at fifteen cents a dozen."

"Ninety cents—two sixty altogether," Joseph figured.

"A load of wood for the blacksmith, two dollars."

"Four sixty," Joseph stated without looking up from his paper.

"Well, when I went to the store to get the things we needed, it came to exactly four sixty, Sabina."

Sabina lifted a big blue milk crock into the large dishpan full of suds and began washing it capably.

"But we owe more tithe than just what we sell, Reuben. We owe tithe on what we eat, and what we use, and all that. Isn't that right? Our increase. Isn't that right, Reuben? The Bible says that belongs to God."

Reuben sat down and dropped his hands into his lap in complete discouragement. Sabina's heart went out to him in pity. His patched denim coat, his rough chapped hands, his silvering hair tore at her heart. She went over and laid her arm across his shoulder.

"Let's not make any more mistakes, dear," she said softly, tenderly.

168

"It's just not there, Sabina. We just don't have enough to pay tithe. Why, that requires a full tenth of our income, and I just can't make the ten tenths stretch now, till we get on our feet a little more."

"But, Reuben, don't you remember, the Bible says, 'Prove me now.' It says if we are faithful, God will pour out a blessing that there will not be room enough to receive. If ever there was anyone needed a few blessings, we do."

Reuben was so tired from his trip to town that he had not bothered to take off his coat or boots. He just leaned back in the high-backed hickory chair and closed his eyes wearily.

"Well, I believe we ought to try it, anyway, and I remember the minister said the nine tenths would go farther than the ten tenths."

"That is not reasonable, Sabina. We have to be realistic, and figures just don't lie."

"You know, Reuben, there is something funny about being a Christian—something you can't just sit down and figure out coldly on paper. I was thinking the other day that it is the only victory we can claim by surrendering. You know, in real war a surrender

169

means defeat. But not with Christ. Surrender means victory."

"Where is that chapter with those promises about tithe, Mother?" Joseph asked.

"Malachi, Son," Reuben answered. "Last book in the Old Testament. Third chapter." The lad got down the big Bible and took it over to the table.

"I never thought of that," Reuben answered. "Those are lovely thoughts. I am very proud of you, dear. You always have been a queen among women. I wish I could do better by you."

"Yes, and another thing. You know, bloodstains are very hard to remove from anything. Yet in the Christian life the blood of Christ takes out stains. We can't reason out some things; they are just true. We find them out and then marvel at them. I believe we would find it so about tithe."

"Here are the texts," cried Joseph from the table where he had been leafing through the big Bible. Since they had moved to Oak Valley, the poverty, hardships, and reverses they had suffered had bound the family together in such a bond of fellowship as is seldom enjoyed under plush and favorable experiences. Sabina told Reuben once that it was worth it all, for it gave them more time to love and enjoy one another.

Then Joseph began proudly to read the wonderful tithing truths and promises as recorded so long ago by the last of the Old Testament prophets.

"And prove me now, herewith," rang out his clear, sweet boyish voice, "if I will not open you the windows of heaven, and pour you out a blessing, that there shall not be room enough to receive it."

"We could do with some of those blessings," Sabina commented cheerfully, bustling about with the finishing touches of supper. "I wish you hadn't bought a thing, Reuben. I wish we'd sit down and figure out what our tithe is and pay it. If God tells us to do a thing, I believe He will open the way for us to do it. I believe that, Reuben."

Reuben was a little irritated. "But, Sabina, I got only the bare necessities—matches, salt, lye, and calico. We *have* to live."

"There's where we can prove God," his wife said earnestly. "If the thing worked out so easy, what would there be to prove?" But Reuben only shook

171

his head. "We've made so many mistakes now that I am fearful of making others."

Young Reuben and Ephraim had come in and were washing at the bench under the towel rack. There was a tin comb case with a small wavery mirror above it where the boys cleaned up for supper. The little girls were playing house with the cat.

"Wash up for supper, girls," Sabina said. She realized that if Reuben had a thing figured out in his head, it was like moving the Rock of Gibraltar to change him. And the sad part of it all was that he was not always right.

"I think——" It was young Reuben who entered the conversation now. Sabina, looking at him, always felt a warm surge of pride. So eager, so earnest, so anxious to order his young life aright. "I think we ought to do as mother says, Father. I have been paying tithe out of the money that I have earned, and I tell you, I think it has paid off already. You know, Mr. North paid me for herding his cattle that time he had to go on a trip? Well, I didn't think I'd get that work any more, for his nephew lives right there in town. But he asked me today to help him again.

172

Then, do you remember the fine coat he gave me that someone gave him while he was away? I figure that that all came because I decided to pay tithe—a blessing He poured out on me, Father."

Reuben sat for a while considering. He had not yet learned to trust his affairs to One who can bring victory out of certain defeat. He had not learned that what is wisdom in God's sight is foolishness to sinners. And so he sat and pondered on the unreasonableness of having more left when you give away a portion.

At last he spoke. "I'll tell you what," he said. "Let's get that little black notebook and keep it and a pencil up there on the clock shelf. We will keep track of the tithe we owe, and we will pay it all off when things begin to break for us. Things will come our way pretty soon. You'll see. There is an old saying, 'It is a long lane that has no turning.'"

Those words were brave, but neither wise nor good. Not a person at the table, even Reuben, but realized it. The family ate silently. The food was plain and good, well-prepared and nourishing, but a shadow had fallen over their usually blithe spirits.

173

Death Stalks the House

*T*HE NEXT YEAR saw harder times than ever. There was a drought of such proportions that the corn crop was a complete failure. Wheat grew in the bottom land, good hard wheat that ripened and was harvested before the dry weather set in. But the price was so low, it hardly paid to take it to market. There was suffering everywhere. The government issued flour, dried beans, and apples in some places. Reuben took some home a little sheepishly, when the storekeeper in the valley offered it to him. He had it fixed up in a basket.

"Here's your portion, Reuben," he said, little sensing the fierce pride and Reuben's independent spirit. "You ain't no beggar, an' we all know that. But your family just as well have some as others who don't work near as hard. It's your gover'ment, too, ya know."

As if it were not enough, that very day while he was gone, Ephraim was thrown from a horse while he was going after the cattle. Benjamin and Joseph saw the horse bolting, and ran as fast as they could to his rescue. They found Ephraim, lying unconscious by the stile that went over the fence into the horse pasture. One arm was crumpled under him, and the blood was pouring from a terrible wound in his temple.

Sabina had been making a little dress for Lily out of an out-moded one of hers, left from the plush days at Conners, when she heard the running feet and the screams. Her heart plunged, and she ran after the two boys till she came to the silent, still heap at the stile. She heard herself screaming one scream after another, then, hearing Joseph begin to scream too, she told herself, "I must not do this. I must be strong; the boys are looking to me. We may save him." Then to the boys she said, "Don't touch him till we get a quilt and ease it under him. Father said that was the rule for the wounded in the battlefield.

Binding up his head, she noted with great joy that he still lived.

Reuben, hitch up the horse to the wagon. Joseph, get the feather bed off somebody's bed—run, now!"

Sabina, lightning quick, had taken off the snowy apron and torn it into strips and knelt by her boy. Binding up his dear head, she noted with great joy that he still lived, and she prayed. Every breath she breathed was a prayer—a prayer so urgent that Sabina told the Lord that she could give up anything, yes, even do anything if He would spare her boy.

She knew only home remedies, but she had good sense. That and prayer had carried her through many a hard situation. Before she hardly realized it, Reuben was there with the wagon, and in the back was a straw tick topped by a feather bed and a wide clean sheet. Joseph had thrown on some pillows, too.

Tenderly, carefully, they rolled the boy onto the quilt, carried him in the hammock it made, and put him into the wagon. Joseph was left with the two little girls, who, oblivious to danger and trouble, were playing house out under the lilac bush in the back yard with broken bits of china and their cats.

The three miles to town seemed interminable. Sabina, white-lipped, and greatly weakened with fear, prayed with every breath and worked over her boy. Oh, if the roads were not so full of ruts! Oh, if they could only get there quicker! Every minute might mean the difference between life and death to her boy. She would not have believed it, but fifty years later, smooth concrete roads and high-powered cars, such as were only in the dreams of the inventors, would cover that distance in three or four minutes of leisurely speed.

Working frantically, she asked herself again and again, "Will he die? Will we have to have this almost unbearable misfortune heaped on top of all the rest?" Why, poverty was an easy load compared with this. Even in all her distraught worry, as she stanched the blood and continually tore fresh strips from one of her voluminous petticoats, which she had now removed, her mind kept reverting to one thing—that little black book on the clock shelf. In it, faithfully written down, was the mounting debt of tithe she and Reuben owed to the Lord. Even little Ephraim here had been more faithful than they. When her mother had sent each of the boys a dollar, they all had taken out their tithe and paid it the next Sabbath at church. All of them were so eager to prove God—except she and Reuben, who should have been the ones to teach the children to walk in the ways of the Lord.

They were just rounding the last curve in the road when she saw Ephraim beginning to move a little. His eyes flew open—hazel eyes, they said, but they were gray with little flecks of brown. His right arm flew up to his head.

"Don't Ephie," Sabina said. "Don't touch your head. You've been hurt. Mother is here."

"Help me, Mother," he moaned—just a small boy again, for all his eleven and a half years.

"Yes, Ephraim, mother will. Only lie still."

"Prince bucked, Mother, he did—scared of a rag that blew down the path. Help me, Mother."

"Yes, Ephraim. Trust mother. We're getting you to the doctor."

Men ran up to the galloping horse and helped to stop the wagon.

Then they helped carry the lad, bed and all, into Dr. Bucklin's office behind the drugstore. Reuben just missed them. He had gone home by the river road. The front of Sabina's buff calico dress was scarlet with blood.

"Don't leave me, Mother," the lad pleaded, even though Dr. Bucklin, who had called in Noah Nelson, the livery stable man, to help him, thought she had better go.

"It's a perty bad break. Be hard t' set. She might go t' pieces," the doctor said to Noah.

"Not Sabiny," Noah whispered. "She ain't that kind. She's got more grit 'n most men. Let 'er stay."

"Mother will be right here," Sabina told her boy.

And stay she did, holding the lad's small brown hand. She talked to him so quietly, so urgently, that even though he was frantic with the terrible pain, he held still. Tears streamed down his rough sun-tanned boyish cheeks, and tears streamed down Sabina's. She would have gladly borne the pain—all of it—if she could. After an eternity—a stretched-out eon—the bone was set, and the frightful wound on Ephraim's head was cleansed and bandaged. He lay back, spent and panting, his eyes betraying the pain. Then Reuben came in, wild with fear; but the doctor put his arm around him.

"I tell you, Reuben, yer boy is saved today because you picked a wife who had sense. I know many a family in this very county who would have lost a boy if they had had to face up to what Sabiny had to face today. He'll live and give you many an anxious moment, I figger."

Dr. Bucklin told all over town that he thought the world lost a first-class nurse because Sabina had not chosen that as her profession. "She's got brains enough t' have been a doctor, too. Mebbe sometime more women 'll take up doctorin'. I dunno."

Reuben told Sabina what the doctor had told him—that she should have been a doctor, or a nurse.

"I am both, lots of times," she said while she superintended the taking of the lad, feather bed and all, and putting them into the wagon. Only after they were in the wagon did Sabina's composure break, and she burst into such a fit of weeping that if old Dr. Bucklin had not been such an old hand at human behavior, he'd have been alarmed. He only climbed right up into the wagon, put his fatherly arm around her heaving shoulders, and sent young Reuben to the town pump after good cold water for her.

181

"That's all right, Sabiny," he said comfortingly. "Get yer cry out, an' you'll feel better. I always say a good bawlin' is good for everyone—once a year anyway."

Sabina was glad that Reuben was along to go home with her. Reuben Junior was allowed to go on home on the horse, but was admonished more than usual to be careful, much to his disgust. Boys of sixteen know a great deal.

Ephraim mended slowly, and the doctor bill, small as it was, added to the burden that was almost heavier than they could bear. Sabina still faithfully wrote down the tithe that they did not pay. Month after month went by, ticking off their lives, until the amount stood at an even three hundred dollars.

Sabina stood looking at the book, then out of the window, where the snow lay deep and the shadows of evening were purple and very cold. The windows looked pretty with the lacy beauty of the frost. Dimly, Sabina wondered what it would be like to be eligible to the outpourings from the windows of heaven. God had never been proved. The time had never seemed favorable.

Death Stalks the Home

One cold snowy day in late February Lily, never a rugged child, came home from school with a chill and a fever. She had pleaded to go to school or Sabina would never have let her go. She was able to read her whole primer through before she ever went.

By night she was breathing so hard that one could hear her across the room. Sabina tried everything she knew—goose grease, turpentine and butter mixed and heated and put on red flannel for her little white throat. She cried for food, but she could not swallow. Sabina made her a little sassafras tea and fed it to her with a spoon. She would not let Sabina leave her side. Reuben and the other boys got the meals and did the work. She did not mend. By the next morning she was so bad that Reuben went out by starlight, saddled the horse, and raced to Oak Valley for Dr. Bucklin. She was dead when the men, covered with snow, pushed through the door. Sabina would not believe it. She was in a stupor and had to be led from the room. The neighbors came in and did the kindly offices for the dead. Food was brought in, and the house was full of kind people, of good people who were anxious to soften the blow.

183

It took a death to heal the breach between Sabina and her parents.

They set Lily's little casket, shaped like the sole of a shoe, on the sofa Reuben and Sabina had bought so gaily for their first home back in Conners. Dear God, they had never dreamed that on its lustrous tufted surface would set the small coffin holding their little Lily flower.

Sabina's mother and father came to the funeral. This was one good thing that had come out of the misfortune. They had been so angry at Reuben that they had never come to see them since they had begun to keep the seventh-day Sabbath. Little Lily had loved her grandma so much. When the door opened to admit the grandparents on the day they buried little Lily, Sabina threw herself into her mother's arms and sobbed and wept over the days and weeks and months of estrangement. It took a death— a deep, terrible sorrow—to heal the breach.

Faithful are the wounds of God. The little new mound that was Lily's grave crystallized Sabina's determination to pay that tithe—pay the current tithe, yes, and all that had been written down in the little black book on the clock shelf. She and Reuben talked it over and both of them decided to prove the Lord.

Sabina Takes a Job

*T*HE VERY NEXT morning after the decision to pay their tithes, Sabina finished up her work and walked the two and a half miles to a small box factory which was operated at the edge of the village to the south of them. (Reuben was clearing the roads with the horse, earning a little extra money; besides, the farm could not spare the one horse to go with her all day every day.) Here at this small factory she applied for work.

"You would not work on Saturday?" the owner asked, watching her closely.

"No," Sabina answered. "But isn't there something I could do the five days of the week?"

"You would not make as much," he commented.

186

"No, but we need the money for an honest debt, and every little bit would help."

After a moment of silence, the manager agreed.

"Come next Monday morning," he said. Sabina felt the hot tears in her eyes as she turned away. She knew that her prayer was answered. She could hardly keep from weeping until she got out of the musty little office of the box factory.

Her pleasure in being able to help was not shared by her husband. He was sick at heart and felt that in some way he had failed her—his brave, good wife, who had been as faithful in the hard days as she was when the way was bright and banked with roses. But now the gray was streaking her hair, and there were lines in the forehead which used to be so smooth and serene. When Reuben took the produce to town that day, he took the tithe out before he bought a thing. Sabina was determined to pry the windows of heaven open—if only just a little crack. She longed for the blessings that she knew would come to reward her faithfulness. That evening they laid out their tithe and got down the little black book. They also paid twenty-five cents on the back

187

tithe. That small entry warmed Sabina's heart more than anything that had happened since they had entered into the new phase of their life. She took it down several times that evening and looked at it. The joy of the whole thing was that the figures for tithes owed would mount no more—no, never! Not for anything would she ever touch the tithe again. Those windows of heaven must be kept open.

The first day at the factory, she was so awkward that it seemed as if her fingers were all thumbs. Reckoning at the end of the day, she found she had made only sixty-eight cents. That seems very small in the light of the present plush times, and even then it was small, but not out of the ordinary. Some unskilled laborers worked for fifty cents to a dollar a day. Schoolteachers worked for thirty dollars a month and were glad to get it. So Sabina was not downcast. Since the factory hands began work at six in the morning in those days, before the wage and hour laws came in, Sabina had to be up long before daylight. The milk was cared for, and the work for the day was started so that it would not be so hard on the children. Ephraim, Rose, and Benjamin did their share and soon learned their parts in the well-organized machinery. Sabina was never late to work.

On her second day she made eighty-one cents. This was a ten-hour day. By the time the first week was up, she was making as much as anyone in the factory. She always said that the Lord lent skill to her fingers. When the first pay was laid in her hands, she mentally calculated offerings. A silver dollar was put in an old sugar bowl on the clock shelf to save for emergencies. It was not to be touched except as the family as a whole decided. That made it fun. And all the rest was paid against the delinquent tithe debt. It took a swift swoop downward, or so it seemed to Sabina. Those few dollars made such a difference.

The whole family gathered around every time the black book was taken out, and Joseph always wanted to do the subtracting. Small wonder that he showed a decided mathematical bent in his later years in school. Reuben always offered a little prayer on these weekly occasions. Then the strangest things happened. Coincidental? No, for too many things happened at once. The cow had twin heifer calves—little beauties they were too. They needed more cattle, for more cows meant more cottage cheese, butter, and milk to trade for necessities. Every one of the turkey eggs hatched, and they had uncommonly good luck with the baby chicks that spring.

Reuben decided to plow the field behind the barn and put it in truck. The whole field west of the barn was planted to melons. They made enough on those two crops to pay off every outstanding debt except the tithe. Reuben got the lumber to build a corncrib.

Then young Reuben got a job making sorghum molasses, adding his bit to the family income. Things were so bright for the family that Sabina did not mind her heavy work program. She was up before the sun every day. The little home ran like clockwork. Everyone had his job and did it cheerfully. Rose, now nine years old, was little house mother. She could bake potatoes, slice bread, and even stir up a batch of corn bread if she needed to. Reuben was proud of his pretty little girl. Sabina made dainty clothes for her from the pretty flowered calico that could be bought for five cents a yard at the store. No little girl at the country school had prettier school dresses.

When Reuben took their sugar cane to the mill where young Reuben was working for old Grandpa Wesling, the old man shook his head.

"I jes' cain't make hit out," the old man said when Reuben came to get his sorghum. "Haint none of the 'lasses I've made 'as got quite the tang yours has. Won't sell it, will ye?"

Reuben sold half of it, so fevered was he to get straightened up and get to living again. He seemed to live for the day when Sabina would quit work. But even though times were better, she would not quit. Though the little ceremony each week saw Reuben's money helping with the debt—even then she fiercely worked on, tirelessly and uncomplainingly through wind and rain and shine. Three years went by. No years of her life went quicker. Every time August the nineteenth came she thought of how old little Lily would have been. "She would have been seven today," she'd tell Reuben. Or, "Little Lily was born eight years ago today. Do you remember how sweet she looked in her little hood the day

191

Aunt Zinnia brought her over to the store for the first time?" No, they could never forget Lily. Even though she was gone, they were glad they had had her. Her memory was ever a great blessing to both of them.

One day, after Sabina had worked for almost three years, Reuben Junior came to her in the kitchen while she was straightening up after supper. "Mother," he said in his quiet way. "Mother, I'm old enough to quit school now, and you can quit working. Father and I don't like to see you work. Let me get a job at the factory and work and you stay at home."

But Sabina turned on the lad, almost severe in her refusal. Nineteen he was, tall, fair, and the very image of his father. "No!" Sabina replied emphatically. Reuben blinked his eyes in amazement. She came and faced her son and put her hands on his shoulders. She had to look up to him now, he was so tall. "No son of mine will——"

Then she went to the clock shelf and showed him the black book. The tithe had all been paid almost a year now. That was what mystified them all.

192

13   "It's for you, Reuben—to go to college on."

"We know all this, Mother," Reuben said. "But what we want to know is, Why are you still working at the box factory?"

The tears were streaming down Sabina's cheeks as she went and rummaged in the top of the old bureau. She drew out a long sandalwood handkerchief box and took a tiny key and opened it. The box was almost full of money. There were gold pieces, silver dollars, and folded bills.

"Why, Mother, what is this for?" the lad asked, marveling not a little.

"It is for you, Reuben—for you to go to Battle Creek College. The thought that you and Joseph and Benjamin and Ephraim and Rose might go has lightened every hour of my work. It was like a text I have read in the Bible. My life seemed to shine 'more and more unto the perfect day.' Just to see my children educated in a wonderful Christian college— yes, and maybe be workers too—would be all I ask to pour out of the windows of heaven."

"But, Mother," the boy protested. "I can't take that—that money. Why, it seems almost like blood money. You walking to and fro all these months and

194

years, and us not helping you as good as we ought to. Father wants to get you a horse."

"Don't say a word." Sabina was laughing through her tears. "You all did your part. No one could ask for more wonderful children than we have. And as for you taking it—there is no question as to that. It will be the happiest day of my life the day you go to Battle Creek."

The boy looked beyond his mother out of the open door. The road wound off to town to his eyes, yet in his imagination it wound on and on and on into a fair land of dreams. Who but precious, patient mother could plan all this and open the door for him, yes, for all of them? Mother was the first to see that the windows of heaven were opened for them all. Father was good, was wonderful, but it was mother who made fabric of dreams. It was she who made you see that the impossible can be achieved.

Sabina jumped to her feet.

"Sunday!" she cried. "My day to get the work 'readied' up for the week, and here I am mooning like a schoolgirl. Fill the boilers with rainwater, Reuben. Joseph, build fires under them in the yard."

195

"What will I do, Mother?" eleven-year-old Rose asked. She was a serious child and did a great deal of work.

"You gather up the clothes, sweetheart. Ephraim, bring me the crock of soft soap in the buttery. Go to the field, Reuben, to help your father as soon as you get the boilers filled. Ephraim can fill the rinse tubs. I'll have this washing on the line before eleven. Want beans and dumplings for dinner, Son?" she asked, smiling, for she knew that was his favorite food.

"Nothing better," the lad laughed, and they all flew to do her bidding like good soldiers under a beloved general.

Ah, how sweet, how lovely was life, thought the young man, and the drawing of the heavy wooden buckets of water from the cistern was as nothing; the joy in his young heart was poignant. The fields seemed covered with a haze of joy to his eyes. Battle Creek College! Even in his wildest dreams, he had not thought it was possible. Ever since the ministers were at their house for a week, spending the nights, and had told them about it, he had dreamed of it, never even confessing his hopes to Joseph or Benjamin.

The ministers had told of the students boarding themselves at first and having an "awful" time. One boy cooked corn meal mush for breakfast, dinner, and supper, until he was never able to eat it again. They told about how a group of them had gotten together and formed a boarding club and made arrangements for some people by the name of Welch to cook for them all.

He would show father and mother that he would be worthy of the sacrifice they were making in his behalf. He would build his life so that no one need ever be ashamed of him. Singing at the top of his voice, he jumped on old Star and rode her at a gallop, bareback, out to the bottom fields where his father was plowing corn.

It took a lot of preparation to get young Reuben ready for the fall term. There was much to do, and Sabina refused to quit work. "I can't do that," she beamed. "If ever we are going to need money, it is now. Besides, I am making more money than anyone else."

197

When youthful Reuben finally stood on the station platform in Oak Valley—with his little bulge top trunk beside him, a telescope valise on the other side, and a well-filled lunch basket in front of him—he felt as rich as King Midas. He knew that packed neatly in the trunk were twelve pairs of yarn socks, two pairs of mittens, one pair of wristlets, and a long knitted scarf; for they had heard that Battle Creek was pretty cold in the winter. There were eight homemade shirts, one Sabbath suit, cut down or rather altered from a fine suit that father had long ago in Conners. Then there was an abundance of everyday things, fresh from Grandma Seymour's needle. There were handkerchiefs, sheets, pillow slips, quilts, and one good wool blanket that grandma had woven herself of wool from their own sheep. Grandma Seymour gave him her Bible, too, a new one that grandpa had bought her. But she told Reuben, "Pshaw, but I can find things ever so much quicker in the old one."

The women spent a lot of time and thought on the food for the trip. It must last him till he reached his destination. There were few fancy places to eat in those days; and as to diners—well, if there had been one on the train he took, he would have rather had what his mother fixed for him than all the dining car food they could pile into a boxcar. There was a lot of good bread and butter, wrapped in fresh cabbage leaves to keep it moist and fresh. There were big apples from the Spitzenburg and the Seek-No-Further trees. There was a tin box full to the brim of cookies made with molasses, hickory nuts, and raisins. Reuben was hungry already at the thought, though he had just gotten up from a big dinner.

The train finally arrived, clanking and clattering and throwing cinders everywhere. The lad climbed aboard importantly, with his trunk check and his money to pay down for tuition stowed carefully in the big wallet that was one Reuben had used. He tucked it carefully in the inside pocket of his coat, having been warned against pickpockets by Reuben, Sabina, Grandpa Seymour, Grandma Seymour, Mr. Hodgens, the station man, Dr. Bucklin, and Noah Nelson. Reuben had to help his oldest son to get all his paraphernalia on board; but he had to get off right away, for the train stopped only a few moments in the small village.

199

The train began to move, and Reuben's white face pressed eagerly against the windowpane soon became a blur. Then as the train rounded the curve and disappeared altogether, they all wept openly. But the tears were not all tears of sorrow for—well— it was hard for Sabina to explain it—but it was as if he was walking out of the door of their lives into a self-sufficiency that would make him no longer dependent on them. They were not sad that this was so. Sabina remembered her boy as he was when he was only a baby, later as a sturdy self-assertive little boy, so independent, so eager to be himself, and to do his little bit. She wept for the beauty that had been hers and would soon belong to others, though she would ever have her mother's share.

Reuben told Sabina and grandpa and grandma on the way home that it should be a day of gladness and rejoicing, a day of pride, a day of gladness that no war had reached compelling fingers out to seize upon young Reuben's tender youth, to devour him. It should be a day of rejoicing that he was a good boy and not like so many others who gave their parents so much worry and sorrow.

Talking like this in his quiet tone, he had them all comforted, and they were laughing and talking naturally by the time they reached home.

"Remember," he said as he stopped by the kitchen door to let them out. "Remember, next year Joseph must go." But through it all, they did have a load on their hearts, for it was Reuben, their first-born son. They were thankful though that it was a Reuben who was not unstable as water, who was going out into the big, cold, unkind world. Sabina knew in her heart that she had lost a boy, for she knew that when he returned, he would be a man. Her carefree boy, dependent on them, would be gone forever.

Reuben and Sabina
Take a Trip

SO LIFE went on. Every day Sabina did her work at the box factory, shaping, folding, pasting. Into every box went the fabric of her dreams, bright and glorious dreams. Through every day, with its hard toil and compelling energy to be spent, was woven the golden thread of a mother's dream, leading on and on into life eternal. A golden thread of love, to tie and bind her dear ones lest they wander and be scattered abroad, lest they be lost.

Miles and miles, through snow and rain and heat and cold, Sabina went to and fro. Reuben worked early and late. Now, every cent they could scrape up went to their children's education. One by one they all went.

Finally, Reuben was graduated and was sent to the Southeast to work, which was not too far from home. Of course the entire family always enjoyed his visits at home, but it was Sabina who secretly rejoiced in her heart whenever she saw Reuben. She often thought of what might have been and was so glad they started paying their tithes.

Later Reuben was married to a girl he met at the college. Sabina treasured every visit home, every letter. She read them over and over. She kept them all in the top bureau drawer, tied with discarded ribbons—treasures the children found years later after she had died.

Rose was graduated from the college the same year that Joseph was ordained to the gospel ministry. Since Reuben and Sabina had not been able to attend Reuben's graduation and ordination, Reuben thought they ought to go now. One of the neighbors promised to care for the livestock and do the milking, so there was no reason why they could not go and see Battle Creek, attend the graduation, and see Joseph ordained. So Reuben and Sabina, now past middle age, took the first long trip they had ever taken

together. Young Reuben and Benjamin and Ephraim
had promised to be there, so it was to be a family
reunion. Benjamin and Ephraim were working for
the food company, and both of them had married.
Reuben and Sabina were to see their grandchildren
for the first time. Reuben now had a little boy, and
Benjamin and Ephraim each had a small daughter.

They carried a food basket on the train, just like
the one they had packed for Reuben several years
before. Each mealtime Sabina laid out the clean tea
towel, the delicious brown bread, the little jars of jam
and jelly, the baked beans, the cottage cheese, and the
cookies, scalloped on the edges, full of raisins and
nuts.

Joseph met them at the station and took them to
the place he had found for them to stay. It was a
room on the second floor of the nurses' dormitory,
across from the sanitarium. They ate in the dining
room at the sanitarium, and Reuben and Sabina
marveled at the wonderful food. Then Joseph took
them out to see the sights. But the greatest thrill of
all came when they were seated in the tabernacle, a
building they had longed to see. And there they

were, with their whole family together in church. Reuben here, with his lovely wife and little boy, from his work in the South. Joseph, who was to be ordained, and who was to work with a seasoned evangelist in the Middle West. Benjamin, who was saving up his money now so that he could take the medical course. Ephraim, who was doing well in the laboratory at the food company. And Rose, lovely Rose, quiet, modest, and sweet, who was already enrolled in the nurses' training course at the sanitarium. Was there ever a family more blessed?

Sabina and Reuben, sitting there, thought of the long, hard road over which they had traveled. They marveled that one small book with a black binding could change the lives of so many people. Where would they all be if they had rashly denied the light as it had come to them so plainly? Indeed, where would they have been if the store they had started so blithely had succeeded? Reuben would have been on the road so much they would have had little time to train their boys in the simplicity and the beauty of holiness. Then, the two of them, graying, and perhaps a little countrified as to dress, thanked God for the sore trials that had come to them through the years.

As they sat there, waiting the solemnity of the ordination service, they glanced around the beautiful tabernacle, called the Dime Tabernacle because so many Sabbath school children sent dimes to help build it. It was full of people, even though it was an afternoon service. Some of the windows were raised and a cool breeze flowed in at the windows.

Just then the brethren came in, with Joseph, solemn, and so youthful looking, in their midst.

After the service was over, they went and stood in the vestibule, waiting for the children to find them. At last, they saw Reuben, tall and strong, coming toward them. Joseph and Ephraim were close behind, and they saw Rose and Benjamin through the crowd. Reuben came up smiling and put his arm around his father's neck. He was half a head taller than Reuben senior.

An elderly man, tremulous with age, saw them looking up into the face of their fine son. Then the others began to gather, and the old man edged near and asked Reuben, "Your children?"

Sabina heard and smiled in her pride and answered, "Yes, our children."

"They are my portion," Reuben answered, "the goodly portion the Lord allotted to me instead of the riches I set out to amass."

The old man nodded. Tears filled his gentle eyes.

"My family are all gone," he said brokenly. "I am alone in my old days. You are so rich—richer than you realize."

"You are right there, friend," Reuben said. "In my youth I set out to find riches and to build my life on a foundation that war nor famine nor political upheaval could mar. I had a lot to learn."

"You did, Father," Joseph told his father. "You built on a sure and true foundation. You and mother both have built surely, and your house need never fall."

As they passed out of the church, Joseph seized his father's arm and leaned over and whispered in his ear.

"There's the man that caused all the trouble, Father." Then he pointed to a brisk, businesslike, bearded man, under average height, limping slightly.

207

"Who caused what trouble?" Reuben responded, his eyes on the vigorous old man, going as swiftly as he could limp down the street.

Joseph laughed. "That is Elder Uriah Smith, Father," he said.

Reuben stopped stock still. "You mean, the man who wrote *Thoughts, Critical and Practical, on the Books——*"

"Yes," Joseph answered. "He wrote the book that——"

"That helped me to find my portion, Son," Reuben said, and they all, with joy in their hearts, thanked God for the portion they all had in the glorious Advent Movement.

TEACH Services, Inc.
P U B L I S H I N G

We invite you to view the complete
selection of titles we publish at:
www.TEACHServices.com

We encourage you to write us
with your thoughts about this,
or any other book we publish at:
info@TEACHServices.com

TEACH Services' titles may be purchased in
bulk quantities for educational, fund-raising,
business, or promotional use.
bulksales@TEACHServices.com

Finally, if you are interested in seeing
your own book in print, please contact us at:
publishing@TEACHServices.com
We are happy to review your manuscript at no charge.

www.ingramcontent.com/pod-product-compliance
Lightning Source LLC
Chambersburg PA
CBHW050359030726
47503CB00006B/1938